D0923921

Perfecting Amiable

A Novel

MARILYN ARNOLD

All Rights Reserved and Assigned to:
Mayhaven Publishing
PO Box 557
Mahomet, IL 61853

Cover Art: Doris Wenzel and Aaron Porter
Cover Design: Aaron Porter
Copyright © 2007 Marilyn Arnold
First Edition - First Printing
ISBN 10: 1-93227823-0
ISBN 13: 978-1-93227823-1
LOC Number: 2006936148

Printed in Canada

Dedicated to my dear friend, Lem Levitt, who knows everything and can do anything. Without him I could neither have cut a house in half nor killed off a flock of turkeys. My weapon of choice is words; his, brains and brawn.

ny Earned

d of : some are grea

rn great, not thrust so

upon great...ss, and h

es...   disc

er

w

ne

ed Penny Ear

d of : some are g

not thru

One

The Carruth house is still there, the back half of it anyhow, where it's always been, set away from the highway out
there on the north end of town. The building has obviously
languished in a divided state for some time. Up close, you
can still make out bits and pieces of what used to be rose-
patterned wallpaper on the wall facing the road. That wall
was on the inside before Thurlin Carruth took a chain saw to
the house some ten or twelve years ago. Strangers who come
through Amiable always remark on the half-house and want
to know where the other half is and why it was divided in
the first place and why nobody's torn the eyesore down. It's
a long story, and the locals prefer to keep it to themselves.

Marilyn Arnold

The town of Amiable was named by the first settlers to the vicinity, an optimistic bunch who were happily afflicted with minimal self-knowledge and a misplaced faith in human nature. What happened in Amiable on the day our story begins was so obvious a smirch on the town and its self-proclaimed amiability that everybody and their dogs turned out to see it. They wouldn't have missed it for the world. As if by appointment, they gathered at sunup, at a safe distance, around the old white frame house that sat peeling its paint serenely in front of a giant cottonwood tree. The unimposing rectangular structure was the joint property of Thoral and Thurlin Carruth, two brothers born less than ten minutes apart, who inherited the place when their elderly parents failed to wake up one morning a few short weeks before. Everyone said how sweet it was that the gentle pair could depart this vale of tears together. No one dreamed of suggesting foul play or collusion. The county coroner and the local pastors gave God the credit, and that was that. They were probably right.

Thoral and Thurlin were in their sixties by this time, but everyone still called them the Carruth boys, most likely because the two had no other siblings and had never lived anywhere except with their parents. Bachelors they were, bachelors and fraternal twins. But fraternal they were not, in any sense beyond the biological. Everybody knew why they weren't, and took great interest in the enmity that festered between the pair. Such enmity went against all the dictates of

Perfecting Amiable

civil society, especially Amiable society; but then, everyone
was familiar with the bad example set by Cain and Abel. The
Carruth brothers had been on the outs for a good forty years,
and yet hadn't budged from home in all those years. The
townspeople couldn't figure out why at least one of them had-
n't bolted, got himself shut of the other. In fact, the topic
afforded many hours of entertainment for the local philoso-
phers when long winter evenings dragged and folks wearied
of complaining about the president and the mayor. (The governor was too bland a figure to generate either anger or praise.)

After the elder Carruths died and the town learned what
Thoral and Thurlin intended to do, they also learned why neither boy left. Not only had each wanted the same girl in the
beginning—which is what started the quarrel and lost both of
them the girl—but in the end, each wanted the house, for himself and himself alone. Well, you couldn't split a girl in two,
despite what King Solomon proposed on one occasion, but
you could split a house. It wouldn't be easy, but you could do
it, once the original owners were deceased. And split a house
was what they intended to do. Split it and move the front half
to a far corner of the property, facing the other direction.
People said the girl's parents moved themselves and her to
Iowa to get her away from the situation, which situation was
causing her to bite her fingernails to the nub and to throw up
after meals. That perception may or may not have been true.
Nobody took Doctor Murphy's affidavit on the matter.

Marilyn Arnold

In any case, the day came when the boys intended to cut the house in half. For just plain excitement in a small town in the middle of nowhere, you couldn't beat an event such as this. The persimmon festival couldn't hold a candle to it. It ranked right up there with barn fires and the births of two-headed calves.

Thoral Carruth was a tall, skinny fellow, like his mother's people, while Thurlin was short and stocky, like his father's. At precisely sunrise on the appointed Saturday morning in early May, Thurlin appeared at the rear door of the house with a large sledge hammer in his right hand. He stood a long minute, gazing around him at the gathered crowd. He was dressed as always, in faded blue bib overalls, a faded chambray shirt, and an old tan canvas hat with a crooked brim. And as always, his prominent jaw carried about three days' growth of salt and pepper beard. Circling the hat's lumpy crown was a bleached band where sweat had dried on the canvas over and over again. Scowling, Thurlin stomped through the weed-choked iris along one side of the house and stopped opposite a crude black X spray-painted on the concrete foundation. Ceremoniously, he leaned the hammer against the building and rolled his sleeves to the elbows. By his actions Thurlin announced that he was ready for, and fully capable of, hard labor. He picked up the sledge hammer, raised it behind his right shoulder with both hands, and gave it a mighty sideways swing. It struck the X dead on, and the crowd winced in unison.

Perfecting Amiable

When Thoral appeared, in his red Yankees baseball cap, striped overalls, and faded red shirt—lumbering slowly up the drive behind the wheel of a rusty yellow backhoe—the towns-folk knew for sure the boys were going to do it. It wasn't just talk. Thoral had appropriated and repaired the backhoe when the department of highways abandoned it next to the cemetery two years earlier. He was a man who planned ahead, as every-body knew. And so there they all were, without breakfast, standing on one foot and then the other, watching Thurlin bang holes in the foundation while Thoral methodically gath-ered up two big leftover utility poles from behind the shed and aligned them with the holes Thurlin was making. This was the first time anyone had seen the boys work in such close prox-imity and with such harmony since they were youngsters. People even speculated that for years the pair had eaten their meals in shifts so as to avoid indigestion and other eating dis-orders associated with brotherly love.

Everybody was eager to see the thing unfold, though they still thought it foolish and a shame that two grown men couldn't go on sharing the family home like reasonable peo-ple. Certainly, the least they could do was pretend to like each other, for the sake of the town and its reputation. After all, there was the welcome sign as you entered Amiable from the west announcing that in Amiable, "friendliness flows in the water." The quarrel was neither a shame nor a mystery to the children of Amiable, however. Being bred from the cradle to be selfish and quarrelsome themselves, most children understand these things instinctively.

Outwardly horrified though inwardly fascinated by what was transpiring, the town watched as Thoral, with surprising dexterity, inched the forward pole toward the forward hole where Thurlin threaded it into the foundation. Directing it out the other side was the tricky part. The watchers assisted by twisting their tongues and necks just so. At last, both poles were threaded through the foundation supporting the front half of the house. The boys secured the poles with ropes across the roof, back and front, while the spectators heaved a collective sigh. The watchers were getting hungry, but they didn't dare go home or even sit for fear of missing something or losing their place. What next? everyone was asking. Old Mr. Hotchkiss became the instant authority, having seen a house moved once, in Nebraska, when he was five years old.

"Got to jack 'er up," he said. "Can't drag her thattaway."

"Got to jack 'er up," the crowd echoed.

Even as these words reached the airwaves, the always clean-shaven Thoral emerged from the shed pushing a large, greasy jack. Thurlin was right behind him with another. No one knew where the Carruth boys got equipment like that, and some of them said they didn't want to know. Ignorance may not be bliss, but it's easy on the conscience and it allows room for considerable moral latitude.

"Ah," the crowd sighed, "jacks."

Perfecting Amiable

At this point, hunger got the best of a few of the older spectators, and they slipped away to take repast during what they judged to be the most tedious and least inspiring part of the operation. The rest held their ground, perhaps on the outside chance that one of the Carruth boys would pick up the sledge hammer and bash the other's brains out with it. At the very least, they might witness a smashed hand or foot if a pole slipped. But as if to spite the faithless, the brothers left the poles and took up the cutting, which everyone who stayed said would be the trickiest and the most interesting part of the process—and the most educational. Why bother to get out of bed if you're going to miss the cutting, they asked each other. Even so, the crowd let out a collective gasp when Thoral stomped out of the shed with a chain saw in one hand and a gas can in the other. Not far behind him was Thurlin with an extension ladder under one arm and a can of oil in his other hand.

"Don't fergit t' turn the power off!" a voice sang out from the crowd.

Thurlin turned and delivered a withering look in the direction of the shouter. That little detail was not something a Carruth would overlook. The crowd backed away from the man who had disgraced himself, so as to dissociate themselves from him. They, of course, would never make such a blunder—especially since they themselves would never have thought of the electricity in the first place. Once the chain saw was properly fueled with the right mix of gas and oil, and the ladder placed against the house, Thurlin climbed the sloping shingles to the ridge of the roof. There, with impressive balance, he measured a certain distance from the front of the building to the middle, chalking a line from ridge to eaves on both sides. Then he nailed a series of small boards, for steps, up one side of the shingled roof and down the other.

At last, donning eye-protecting goggles, he signaled Thoral for the chain saw and lugged it to the ridge. There he rested it across the ridge beam and pulled the starter rope. The machine sprang to life, nearly throwing Thurlin off the roof. He uttered a few well-chosen words, some of them entirely new to a few women in the audience, braced himself, and applied the saw to the ridge at his chalk line. Down he moved, cutting from top to eaves, playing no favorites, dividing his time equally among spectators on either side of the house. In the meantime, Thoral had been measuring and chalking lines down both side walls. That finished, he went for his old Dodge pickup, which he intended to use as a platform for reaching the upper walls of the one-story structure. He parked it on the side opposite the ladder, among the chrysanthemums and the weeds.

People were amazed at how smoothly the whole thing went, each man seeming to know his assignment in advance, each having a vested interest in a successful outcome. A few of the onlookers had been secretly hoping for trouble between

Perfecting Amiable

the two brothers as the project proceeded, perhaps a slip-up that each would blame on the other. It was too much to hope that something would happen to ruin the house entirely, although some who had missed their breakfast thought the brothers owed them that much for their sacrifice. When the firehouse whistle blew at high noon, as it had every day but Sunday for seventy-five years, the brothers wiped their hands on their overalls and went in the back door of the house. The folks positioned at the front of the gathering were reluctant to surrender their places, even for lunch, but in the end elected to take sustenance in order to see the event through to the end. It wouldn't do to faint at a critical moment.

At precisely 1 p.m. the brothers reappeared, one from the front, the other from the rear of the house. Apparently, each was already claiming his territory. Wheels and blocks—mainly railroad ties—were brought from the shed, and work began with the jacks to raise the poles and that section of house above them. Methodically, the brothers worked, cranking the house up inch by inch, pushing the blocks in under the poles. And one by one the townspeople arrived, picking their teeth and jockeying for position. Finally, the last of the blocks were placed at the two corners nearest the cut, stacked high enough now for installation of wheels on the ends of the poles. Then the two brothers steered their jacks to the front corners and repeated the process. As they were preparing to lift the poles and insert the last blocks, something went wrong.

Marilyn Arnold

Thoral was in front of the house when the raised section shifted a little and one of the stabilizing ropes around its middle, going from front to back, snapped. He hollered, and Thurlin rushed to see what had happened. After tying the two ends together, they decided to run another rope from top to bottom around the house. There was space enough to crawl underneath now that it stood on blocks. What they had not realized was that one stack of support blocks extended over their grandparents' old root cellar. Having no use for the cellar, their father had covered the hole with a few planks and thrown dirt over it. Before long, weeds and grass hid any evidence of what was beneath.

While the brothers were under the house working with the rope, the planks over the root cellar gave way beneath one front corner of the house. The structure teetered for a second or two before the other stacks of blocks wobbled and collapsed. Then, as if orchestrated, the side walls caved in, with the roof not far behind. Only a section of the front wall remained standing. There was no rear wall to this half of the house because the cut had left the rear open. The back half of the house was intact, firm on its foundation, benignly displaying flowered wallpaper and a picture of John the Baptist prophesying in animal skins.

The townspeople got more than they bargained for that day. The last thing they wanted was for the Carruth brothers to be buried alive, but it appeared that was just what they got. There were no jokes now, no sarcastic remarks about the ill-conceived enterprise or the foolish pride that had crushed two brothers. Children were sent to bed without supper. Adults of every faith or no faith congregated at the local Church of the Brethren Revitalized to console and be consoled. Dogs howled and slunk about, trying to make themselves invisible. Joining in the general lamentation were cows that didn't get milked and pigs that didn't get slopped. People who had forgotten how prayed that night, prayed in their bedrooms and their barns. Folks in these parts generally died of old age and the diseases that accompany it, or maybe someone would get shot by his best friend on a hunting trip, or some wild teenager would meet death in an automobile. These were normal kinds of things. The deaths of Thoral and Thurlin Carruth were not normal. Nobody in this town had ever had half a house land on him that shouldn't have been cut in half in the first place.

This event fell outside the pale of familiar tragedies, and it touched every household. Several men spoke of organizing a crew to search for the bodies and to clean up the tangled mess of shingles, wood siding, and plaster. As if under an hypnotic spell, several men falteringly circled the pile of debris, moving a few boards and calling out "Thoral" and "Thurlin." They got no response and backed off. After all, who could survive having a house drop on him? No one held out hope that either brother could be alive, and most regarded the collapse of the house as an act of God that mortals should let be. In any case, better wait until Monday, people said. It would be sacrilege to disturb the bodies today, while the spirits might still be hovering about; and tomorrow was the Sabbath. One timid fellow did raise the question as to whether removing the house from the fallen brothers would qualify on the standard of rescuing an ox from the mire, but he was shouted down.

Even when the cleanup and search for remains concluded on the half of the Carruth house turned to shambles, nobody would touch the half that still stood, its naked interior wall exposed to the world. There seemed to be a kind of mutual consent to leave it there, as a reminder. The city fathers condemned the property and took possession of it. There were no heirs to dispute the action, so it went uncontested. Some might think the story logically ends here, but it doesn't. The real story, the story of how that ill-fated house eventually changed Amiable, or at least some of its citizens, begins here.

Incidentally, the remains of the brothers were not found immediately. That led to speculation by the town's alarmists that wild animals dug in there at night and carried them off. Another theory held that the remains were pushed deep into the soft earth of the crawl space where they disintegrated instantly, perhaps by divine edict. A traveling evangelical preacher who had a way of turning up at times both opportune

Perfecting Amiable

and inopportune said he'd had a vision of the brothers being carried off by devils. Until now, folks in these parts hadn't put much stock in this particular preacher's opinions, but his explanation of the disappearance won him a few champions—among the very young and the very old. Of course, people who didn't hold to any of these theories kept digging in the rubble and eventually found the bodies and quietly buried them. It must be said, however, that powerful arguments were made for leaving the quarrelsome brothers where the broken house had covered them.

The Carruth house fell on a Saturday, as was noted, and a little memorial service was held at the site on Sunday evening. Sunday morning, however, was not wasted. Predictably, the townspeople turned out for worship in record numbers, to placate their consciences and to hear of their individual and collective complicity and guilt. Always at the ready, local preachers and pastors took the golden opportunity handed them by the Carruth debacle to harrow the souls of their congregations. Did anyone try to stop the brothers from literally dividing their house? No. Did more than a few try for a reconciliation between the brothers? No. Did any of them bear enmity toward the brothers? More than a few. The spiritual shepherds of the various little flocks in Amiable had a powerful object lesson handed to them, and they made the most of it. After all, they now had a concrete illustration of the truisms that a house divided against itself cannot stand and pride goes before destruction.

Owen Prattly, pastor of the Church of the Brethren Revitalized, told his parishioners that the town itself was a "house," their house, and its citizens must be united in faith and brotherhood. The church, too, was a house, he said, united in faith and love. "Don't you dare take a chain saw to this town or this church!" he thundered, and the congregation shrank from the blast, vowing not to take a chain saw to the town or the church even if they had one—or a sledgehammer either. He urged members of his congregation to look on the remaining half of the Carruth house as a dire monument to love's failure, and some of them actually did.

The bishop of the local Mormon ward, Merton Slater, told his congregation that the divided Carruth house symbolized each of them, and the destructive divisions within themselves. "Are we, in actuality, what we profess," he demanded, "or are we one thing on the outside and another on the inside? Let the Carruth house suggest to us the whited sepulcher of hypocrisy that threatens our own souls," he urged. Normally, this kind of talk rolled right off the backs of the good folks of Amiable, who, while excluding themselves, could always think of several others to whom the message applied. This time, however, something stuck and rankled, like an invisible cactus sliver in the big toe of the conscience. And there, too, was the house, inescapable,

18

Perfecting Amiable

preaching its own silent sermon. That night, somebody removed the "Welcome to Amiable" sign from its moorings and nailed it to the front of the remaining half of the Carruth house. The next night somebody tore it off and dumped it at the landfill across the highway.

Two

This is remote country, populated mostly by turkeys, cows, and a variety of wild creatures, in the heart of Utah's mountain-ringed high central desert. Life is so hard here, far from any city of measurable size, that the incredible beauty of the landscape is largely lost on livestock and human inhabitants alike. The folks in Amiable take their lean pleasures where they can find them, rejoicing in each other's small triumphs and minor catastrophes. By and large, they are decent, law-abiding people. When real tragedy strikes, they are there to comfort and console each other, and to bring casseroles. But like all of us, they have their weaknesses, their character flaws—many of those flaws stemming from

Perfecting Amiable

the first and deadliest of the seven deadly sins: pride. And for some reason, such flaws tend to blossom in plain view in small towns where everybody knows and minds everybody else's business. And where people tend to measure the failings of their neighbors against their own virtues.

The fall of the Carruth house hit the town pretty hard. Adults spoke in low voices, and children went to bed and ate asparagus and blew their noses without argument. But as the years went by, the divided house became a commonplace, like the landfill, and folks scarcely noticed it any more. Local churchmen stopped referring to the house and people more or less returned to their old ways. Travelers passing through judged Amiable to be made up mostly of regular folks— allowing "regular" some room for interpretation—and by and large it was. Then one day odd things, mysterious things, small unobtrusive things, began happening in Amiable. These were not threatening things, nor were they hurtful things, and they involved only one person at a time. But little by little the climate started changing in some households in Amiable.

One of Amiable's "regular" folks is the librarian, Coral Agnes Watters. She has aged some since the collapse of the divided house, but she is still the librarian. Coral was the first of several to be singled out for participation in what seemed a strange, unprecedented experiment. She was a good woman, by most standards, but she ran the library in a manner that might have surprised people from elsewhere.

Marilyn Arnold

For instance, even though the library was supposed to be open from 9 a.m. to 2 p.m. on Saturdays, she left it locked up tight without so much as a sign on the door if she had business elsewhere—which she had on the day of the house-cutting. There she was at the Carruth place, a short, stocky, blonde woman with a slightly bent nose, elbowing her way to the front row of spectators because she allowed as how the taller ones could see over her. She ignored the frowns and the clearing of nearby disgruntled throats.

Nobody questioned Coral in those days because she had sovereign jurisdiction over a number of things besides books, and that's how she got people into the library and got them using their library cards, thereby assuring continued funding from the county. In those days, her budget allotment, including the line item of her salary, was based on the average number of patrons that used the Amiable library weekly. Less creative librarians in other towns were envious of Coral's numbers and suspected her of cooking the books, as they say, but she didn't. As many people as she reported did, in fact, walk through her doors, choose something to borrow, and run their cards through her primitive scanner. She had proof of patronage. You can't argue with a machine and get anywhere.

It was a great advantage, of course, that the county seat was nowhere near Amiable, and that the town had only one librarian. Coral made all the decisions and introduced all the innovations. What no outside auditor bothered to review was

Perfecting Amiable

just what items Coral's patrons were checking out of the little library, in addition to the occasional book or tape. Local residents were actually surprised, even pleased, at Coral's creativity. Her former classmates attested that she hadn't been all that bright a light in the public school system. Perhaps English and math classes hadn't tapped into her brand of genius, or perhaps she was merely a late bloomer.

What Coral did was invest the money she collected in fines in a few commodities that some users found more convenient to borrow than to own. Take fishing poles and tackle boxes, for instance. Suppose Bern Trumpla's cousin came to town with no thought of going fishing before he got there. Then when he got there he wished he had brought the fool pole along. Well then, Bern, who ran the Stopover Motel on the east end of town, would just pop into the library and walk out with the necessary equipment under his arm. (Coral did not, however, provide worms. She had her standards, and her limits.) It was common knowledge that a library card issued through Miss Coral's facility was the next best thing to cash in Amiable. Maybe that's why Ace Rents never moved in. How can you beat free?

The previous summer Coral had invested in croquet and badminton sets, though she finally had to insist that users provide their own birdies. The library's feathered missiles had a way of disappearing down wells and onto rooftops. After that, the Amiable Mercantile carried them, cleverly displaying them next to the bird seed and fertilizer. Then last winter Coral stocked a few pairs of snowshoes and ice skates. Naturally, she also lent out a variety of audio and videotapes, along with a few CDs and DVDs. She imposed a heavy fine for the late return of any items, including books, and people paid it to keep their borrowing privileges. Coral loved raking in the money. Even though it wasn't hers personally, she felt a proprietary attitude toward it.

Technically Miss Coral Watters was a Mrs., but people always thought of her as single, even when her husband Derwood was alive. Probably, they thought of her that way because everybody had called her Miss Coral since anybody could remember. Some people even said it wouldn't surprise them a bit if she up and lent Derwood out with the hedge trimmers. No one knew how she felt about Derwood, who was practically old enough to be her father, because in some ways they were a perfect fit. Hardly anybody else could have lived with either of them. They pinched pennies until the copper wore off.

Each of them also had a sweet tooth that rivaled their rage for frugality, and when it got the best of them, they stopped in at the Grab Sum Grub for a piece of apple pie. This indulgence required an outlay of cash, but Coral and Derwood generally came out all right in the bargain. It was a matter of timing and agility. When Dutch Lorimer, owner of the eatery,

Perfecting Amiable

saw them heading his way, he'd rush around emptying the jars containing packets of sugar, cream, and salt. If Dutch was too slow, Coral emptied them for him, into her oversized handbag, along with paper napkins, toothpicks, and exit mints. Dutch always wondered why she left the pepper packets, the ketchup bottles, and the tabasco sauce. Coral could have told him she didn't like pepper even if it was complimentary, and she didn't take the ketchup and the tabasco sauce because that would be stealing. She was not a thief.

Not many people had occasion to call on Coral and Derwood. The locals knew there was no point in trying to collect for the cancer drive, or the Boy Scouts, or any other worthy cause—unless wrinkled napkins and small packets of salt were an acceptable contribution. For a good while Coral made it a point to offer those things, to salve her conscience. "If they're too fussy to take what we offer, then they can just do without," she used to tell Derwood. The Watters house wasn't a place anyone would want to visit anyway, unless he was in the house demolition business. The word "sparse" wouldn't do it justice. "Bare" goes a little too far—but only a little. The front room ceiling light in the small, brown brick house with the sloping porch was a single 75 watt bulb hanging on a cord in the middle of the room. One tarnished floor lamp leaned precariously against a lumpy green overstuffed chair. There were a couple of threadbare throw rugs, one under a wobbly coffee table in front of a sagging brown sofa.

Marilyn Arnold

If some traveling salesman, or promoter, or politician were canvassing the town, children instinctively gathered around the Watters house, at a discreet distance behind hedges, shrubs, and trees, and waited for the show. They were never disappointed. Not even when that fellow soliciting non-perishable items for the state and county food banks stopped at the Watters house. He accepted the salt and sugar packets, leaving Coral so dumbfounded she could do nothing but give them to him. After that, she never gave a solicitor the option. She wouldn't make the same mistake twice. In church, when the collection plate came to her and Derwood, she became occupied with something she had dropped on the floor, or she had a coughing spell, or she was suddenly moved to tears. Every now and then she lapsed into a visionary trance that lasted until the collection plate left her row.

Conversations about the couple, across dinner tables or quilting frames, were likely to go something like this:

"That Coral is so stingy I'll bet she saves fingernails."

"Well, Edna Fay, that may be stretching it, but I seen a box in her kitchen once that had written on it 'string too short to use.'"

Even so, Coral and Derwood had their defenders—mainly people who were a bit tightfisted themselves. Elja Nexel, for example, who regularly stretched an extra week or two out of a perm and had been caught darning a sock, was likely to put in a word for her neighbor.

Perfecting Amiable

"Don't be too hard on Coral," she'd say. "Remember how she's kept the library open when some of them other libraries have closed down? Where else could we borrow all that stuff for free? Why, without her we'd have to *buy* lots more. Some say she's miserly. I prefer to say she's extra prudent. Maybe a trifle cold-hearted, I grant you that. But only a trifle."

Even Elja Nexel had trouble explaining away what Coral did when Derwood dropped dead on the living room floor one spring afternoon, just after he finished reading the day-old paper he regularly recovered from a neighbor's trash bin. The long-time residents of Amiable remember only too well what transpired the day he died. Some were scandalized, her defenders and her detractors in particular; but those indifferent to her, or who had little commerce with the library, just shrugged and said, "That's Miss Coral for you. Prudence before sentiment."

Derwood Paul Watters keeled over with no warning while Coral was in the kitchen scraping carrots for supper. She always said peeling them wasted too much of the good. Hearing a little cry and a thunk, Coral rushed to the living room and found Derwood on the floor. She took his pulse and listened for his breathing. When she was certain he was gone, she rescued the keys to their old Dodge truck from his jacket pocket and made a beeline for the Citizens Bank where she and Derwood had joint savings and checking accounts. The library was closed, but the bank was still open. Amiable may be one of the few places in America where librarians have better hours than bankers. Coral closed out both accounts, emptied the safe deposit box, and drove home. Then she called Amo Milby, the local mortician, and told him to come and get the body. When the mortician reached the house, he could tell that Derwood was not brand-new dead. But at the time nobody could swear on a stack of Bibles that Derwood had died before Coral cleaned out the joint accounts, so they let it go. It was only after the bank teller, Lula Greene, heard about Derwood's death that she put two and two together. Once she had, however, she wasted no time sharing her arithmetical hypotheses with the citizenry of Amiable. Two days later Coral reopened the accounts in her name.

Coral was not a woman who hesitated when time was of the essence. She had heard horror stories about probate court, and she firmly believed in the old saying that he who hesitates is lost. She, in this case. Coral gave the saying her own interpretation and rescued the living money before attending to the needs of a man to whom a couple of hours didn't mean a thing. Furthermore, she reasoned that burial details would not interest him in the slightest. In this frame of mind, and if it had been allowed, she would have buried Derwood in the back yard next to the chicken coop, which had been chickenless for years, and so had lost any objectionable remnants of fowl occupancy. She hated to spend money on a dead person who could hardly appreciate the expenditure. In the end, in defer-

Perfecting Amiable

ence to the town's sensibilities—not to mention the law—
Coral had Derwood planted in a pine wood box in the skimp-
iest part of the cemetery. The citizenry had their opinions
about that, but not because they had any particular concern for
Derwood himself. They figured he'd have done the same
thing in her shoes. The Watters had no children, and it was
several days before Coral took the trouble to call Derwood's
brother in Ohio—collect—to give him the news.

Years went by, and life for Coral settled more or less into
a regular pattern, divided between collecting fines at the
library and pinching pennies at home. Then one early spring
night, a decade or so after the Carruth boys were extracted
from the wreckage of their pride and buried properly, Coral
Watters strolled out onto her front porch at about 11 p.m. The
porch floor hadn't been painted since Derwood died, and neither had the house. The place had slipped because Coral was
not about to pay someone to do what Derwood could have
done if he had been around and in the mood to spend the
money for cheap paint. At the moment she had her eye out for
somebody hot to perform community service. There were few
things Coral hated more than spending money. That had not
changed. Just that day, for example, she had accused one of the
girls at the Merc of short-changing her on a bottle of dish soap.

Coral's chief entertainment in the evenings was going
through her bank statements and totaling up the modest

balances—CDs, money markets, savings bonds, annuities. She was grateful that Derwood had come into the marriage with a pre-paid life insurance policy, a gift from his parents. Coral hated to admit it, but she missed Derwood, especially at night. They hadn't been what you'd call close, but she was used to him. She never went to bed early because she had difficulty sleeping, and this night was no exception. When she opened the warped aluminum screen door for a breath of air, a piece of paper fluttered to the porch floor.

"What's this?" She stooped to retrieve the fallen paper, groaning and reaching for her back when she stood up. Coral's back had been bad for years, but she was not, as she said, going to pay some quack doctor for something like that. "No sense throwing good money after a bad back," she used to say, chuckling at her joke. "Besides," she always added, "I have better things to do with my money." People wondered what those better things were because they were never visible. Some of the more cynical suggested that the only thing Coral did with her money was count it. Muttering to herself as she unfolded the paper left at her door, Coral crossed the worn planks of her living room floor, kicking up a corner of an ancient throw rug as she went. The old floor lamp was still there, its yellowed shade tilted so as to cast the optimal amount of its meager light on the lumpy chair that had supported it for a good many years.

Coral dropped heavily into the chair, reached into her

Perfecting Amiable

lavender seersucker robe pocket for her reading glasses, and peered at the message penciled in capital letters on the inside of the paper. One might think that a librarian would be an avid reader and would therefore have finely crafted eyeglasses. Not Coral. Her glasses came from the bargain table at Woolworth's in Salt Lake City fifteen or twenty years earlier. She fell into the job of librarian not out of a love of books, but because she had some filing experience and because at the time nobody else wanted it. In her view, ninety-nine per cent of the books for adult readers were written by bleeding heart liberals and fell into one of four categories: frivolous, immoral, depressing, or incomprehensible. Of the four, she preferred frivolous if she had to choose. Perhaps it was her general distaste for books that led her to undertake projects that gave new meaning to the term "lending library."

The bold lettering of the note left at Coral's door was readable even in the dim light. This is what it said:

BELOW IS A MAXIM ADAPTED ESPECIALLY FOR YOU. IT CONTAINS A RIDDLE. IF YOU SOLVE THE RIDDLE, YOU WILL RECEIVE A GREAT TREASURE. TO SOLVE THE RIDDLE, GO ALONE AND IN SECRET TO THE DIVIDED CARRUTH HOUSE AND PONDER THE MAXIM. IF YOU DON'T SOLVE IT ON THE FIRST VISIT, RETURN AND PONDER IT AGAIN. DO NOT GIVE UP UNTIL YOU UNDERSTAND THE MAXIM AND ITS APPLICA-TION TO YOU PERSONALLY. WHEN YOU HAVE SOLVED THE

Marilyn Arnold

RIDDLE, WRITE ITS MEANING ON A SMALL PIECE OF PAPER AND TUCK THE PAPER SECURELY OUT OF SIGHT AT THE CAR-RUTH HOUSE. THEN GO HOME AND BEGIN TO LIVE WHAT YOU HAVE LEARNED. HERE IS THE SAYING:

PENNY PRIZE AND FOUND FOOLISH

Coral rubbed her eyes and read the note again. She was only moderately superstitious, while Derwood had avoided ladders and black cats all his days. "What's this all about?" she muttered aloud. "It makes no sense. Who on earth left it anyhow? Some nut case, no doubt. Well, if they think I'm going traipsing down to that ghost house and sit around 'pondering' some nonsense, they're sadly mistaken." She wadded the paper, pushed up out of the chair, and deposited the crumpled message into the brown paper bag that served as a garbage can in the kitchen. Then she went resolutely to bed.

An hour later, unable to sleep, Coral crawled from a tumbled bed and made her way to the kitchen. Switching on the light above the sink, she poured herself a small glass of milk and cast her puffy eyes on the garbage bag. After a minute or two, she slammed the empty glass (it was plastic and said "Travelodge" on the side) on the old wooden counter top and fished the message from the garbage bag. It had acquired a few stains and the faint odor of old orange peels. Coral spread it out on the counter top and tried to smooth its wrinkles with

Perfecting Amiable

her palms. Even without her glasses, she could make out the words. She slowly articulated them: "Penny prize and found foolish." Then she crumpled the paper again. "Ridiculous!" she exclaimed, pitching it into the brown bag and returning to bed, where she lay awake fuming the rest of the night.

The next morning, Coral retrieved and discarded the paper at least three times. All before breakfast. So preoccupied was Coral that she nearly forgot about the library and was, in fact, forty minutes late opening the doors. Throughout the day, she made just about every mistake that can be made in a library—stamping some books out that should have been stamped in, forgetting to run cards through the scanner, hanging the badminton racquets where the fishing poles went, doubling some fines while halving others, sending little children to adult books and thin people to diet books, sending women to the men's room and men to the tiny chairs in the children's reading area. People shook their heads and whispered to each other that Coral Watters had finally cracked. And maybe she had. By closing time, Coral figured she had dreamed the whole thing.

Among those persons now living in Amiable who arrived after the Carruth house-breaking was a woman who had moved into a small house on the east edge of town, back under some hoary old cottonwoods. No one knew where she came from or how old she was, though they knew she wasn't young. Except for trips into town for the things her garden didn't provide, she didn't socialize a great deal. Sometimes, however, she could be seen in the bank or the library, or sitting on the bench in front of the Amiable Mercantile with a wry smile on her face that some folks found worrisome. On her excursions to town, she wore a wide-brimmed straw hat, a long black dress, and a loose white shawl. At first when she appeared, little children hid behind their parents' legs, and dogs barked from the other side of the street. People said she could interpret dreams and cast spells. Some thought she was a witch. Then people got used to her.

Coral Watters was tempted to pay the woman a visit, on the supposition that the woman could dispel the demon that was haunting her. Coral was hesitant because she had pretty much avoided the woman except when she came into the library. Everyone who was anyone avoided her. Maybe it was because she was said to have cats. Older women with cats make people nervous. Nonetheless, the woman seemed at ease moving about town, and appeared to know everyone, almost too well. She called herself Mrs. Ransom, and she checked out books that nobody else ever looked at—books by Greeks and Russians and Germans, and Frenchmen given to a variety of indiscretions—all acquired before Coral's tenure in the library. Mrs. Ransom was not interested in the bestseller list and she claimed to like poetry. That alone made her suspect in Coral's mind because nobody in

Perfecting Amiable

Amiable liked real poetry except Leon Cremm, and he was an outsider. People did, however, prove their erudition by applauding enthusiastically at the Fourth of July picnic when Eddie Gertz read his annual patriotic poem about firecrackers and hotdogs.

Leery about Mrs. Ransom or not, Coral had a problem, and maybe she needed a witch to solve it. She nearly went home to check her garbage bag one more time before driving out to Mrs. Ransom's, but she decided against it. If she did dream the note, checking would only confuse the issue. Besides, she had the saying memorized, and she knew the gist of the rest. Mrs. Ransom's house, which was more a cottage than a house, huddled close to the ground. Coral expected to see forbidding spider webs hanging about the front porch and a big raven giving her the evil eye from the eaves. Not to mention black cats on the railings and tarantulas waiting for victims under the steps. On the contrary. All was tidy, and the only cat visible was a fat yellow one lazing in the window sill. He lifted his head, gazed at Coral for a moment, yawned broadly, and resumed passivity. She hesitated, then stepped boldly to the door. A delicate little woman of fine features and a long chin answered Coral's knock.

"Yes, Mrs. Watters?" the woman said. "What is it you want?"

For a moment Coral lost her nerve. The woman remembered her name! "Uh, Mrs. Ransom? Well, uh, I wanted you to know that we got some new books th' other day, on some of them Chinese poets you asked about."

Mrs. Ransom adjusted her shawl. "Oh, is that all? Won't you come in, dear? I think you have something else to ask."

"Well, 'sa matter of fact, maybe I do. Maybe. Can't we just talk a minute out here, in them chairs?" Coral pointed to two old wicker chairs with faded flowery cushions at one end of the porch. She did not want to go into the house where the rest of the cats might be lurking. Cats in tight quarters made her fidgety.

"Of course, dear. Now, what's troubling you?"

Coral sat, but she remained on the edge of her chair, ready to retreat at the first leap of a cat. "Well," she began, "last night I had this dream. Leastways I think it was a dream. I just left the library, so I haven't been home to double check. I thought maybe you could interpit it for me."

Mrs. Ransom smiled. "Maybe I can, maybe I can't. What was this so-called 'dream' about?"

"Well, it wasn't your standard kind of dream. Somebody stuck a piece of paper in my door—I mean I dreamed somebody did—with a bunch of instructions on it. I'm supposed to take myself over to the Carruth house and set there and think 'til I solve this riddle, and then I'll get a treasure, and it's all pretty spooky, if you ask me. I thought that since you've read all them psychology books, about dreams and suchlike messages from the universe, you could clue me in."

Perfecting Amiable

Mrs. Ransom nodded her head. "I see." She paused. "I've always placed great stock in such events. Acting on these metaphysical, or even physical, promptings can lead to flashes of insight and wisdom."

"Then you think I should do what the paper says, even if I maybe only dreamed the paper?"

Mrs. Ransom smiled again. "Absolutely, so long as you are not told to do anything evil or harmful or illegal. What have you to lose? From the sound of it, you could stand to gain a great deal."

When Coral got home from Mrs. Ransom's, she made a beeline for the garbage bag. The paper was there. She hadn't dreamed it. Unless, of course, she was dreaming it again. Now what was she to do? In a flash, Coral decided to hustle over to the Carruth house and start pondering. The sooner she got started, the sooner she'd be done with it. Coral, who had never pondered five minutes, much less two hours, in her life, was not entirely sure how a person went about it, but figured she'd soon find out. First, she'd better look the word up in the dictionary, to make sure she did what it said pondering was. These things can be a little slippery for someone who wasn't experienced with words, but only with the outsides of books. Now she wished she had spent more time reading during slow periods at the library. Of course, balancing her check book, counting the petty cash, and

perusing the Sears catalogue (not that she'd ever buy anything unless it was at least seventy per cent off) was time-
consuming; and where else could she find the time and the
strength to do those things if not at work?

Focusing now on the "treasure" aspect of the message,
Coral packed a sandwich and an apple, loaded a broken
down webbed folding chair in Derwood's pickup bed, stuffed
the message in the front pocket of her elastic waist stretch-
able blue denims, and drove to the Carruth house. She pulled
way up in the driveway and around the shed. The last thing
she wanted was to have somebody spot her at the abandoned
house, or anywhere for that matter, pondering. If word got
out, she'd be a laughing stock. She might even be shipped off
to the nuthouse and never get the treasure. And maybe not
her Social Security when she became eligible either.

Coral steadied the chair against the back steps of the
remaining half of the building and commenced to do what her
research told her pondering was. That is, she ran over the riddle in her mind—"Penny prize and found foolish." It was the
most idiotic thing she had ever heard. If it applied to her, she
couldn't see it. What kind of a prize would a penny be to anyone but a two-year-old? And even then, it was doubtful. A
dime, maybe, but not a penny. Then again, maybe that was the
"found foolish" part. A penny certainly was a foolish prize.
There was no wisdom to speak of in that. Where was the riddle? How could she, a professional librarian and therefore by

Perfecting Amiable

nature more knowledgeable than the general run of the population, take any lesson from such a trifling statement?

So far as Coral could see, the saying didn't offer much food for thought. And neither did the Carruth house. There it stood, radiating gloom. Why on earth was she instructed to come to this sorry place to do her pondering? Just being here gave a person the willies. If she had to ponder, wasn't there a better place for it than here in the overgrown grass and weeds? Why couldn't she have done it just as well at home, or even at the library? Nonetheless, in a show of good faith and to prove she was as open-minded as the next person, Coral sat there on the property of the fallen brothers with her eyes squeezed tight for a good twelve minutes. Then her left knee began to itch. She was afraid to scratch it for fear of breaking the spell and having to start pondering all over again. Not that there was much of a spell to break. Soon the itch traveled to her left shoulder and then to the unreachable center of her back. To make matters worse, her nose became stuffy and she had no tissue. Finally, she gave up and went home. But she left the chair—just in case.

Coral repeated the performance several more times over the next week, with similar results. The business was starting to get to her, and she was about to wash her hands of the whole affair. "Somebody's playing games with me," she said Sunday morning. "There's no meaning and no treasure." Determined only to pick up her chair, Coral drove one last time to the Carruth house. There had been rain the night before, and the earth seemed washed clean. The sun, just emerging from huge foaming clouds, touched every wet leaf, every weed, every blade of grass. Coral smiled in spite of herself at seeing the natural glitter, especially the bright pinks and reds and whites of untended hollyhocks at the far corner of the house. She always thought of hollyhocks as weeds, mainly because some rather trashy neighbors had them at the bottom of their porch stairs when she was a child. The girls made dolls of them, but Coral never joined in. She was not a "let's pretend" sort of person. She insisted on real dolls that did not wither in their fragile gowns.

Something urged Coral, though, toward the hollyhocks and she left her chair, pulled by their common radiance. "Why, they're beautiful, aren't they!" she exclaimed. "Will you look at that! How come I never thought so before?" She plucked a pink blossom, in full bloom, and then one that had already spent itself, twisting in an upward swoop like the hair of a beautiful lady or a princess. Carefully inserting the short stem of the full blossom into the "head" of the spent one, Coral recreated the neighbor children's illusion of so many years ago: a beautifully coiffed princess in her elegant gown. Coral Watters smiled. It felt strange to her. She realized how long it had been since she had smiled out of pure pleasure.

Coral walked slowly back to her chair, the delicate lady balancing in her left hand. She sat there a long time, gazing at

Perfecting Amiable

the lady, wishing she had made such ladies when she was a child, and that she had played with the unwashed, ill-fed children who aeons ago had seen the magic in a weed. "I wonder," she said aloud, "I wonder if Thoral and Thurlin Carruth saw these hollyhocks, if they grew and bloomed back then." After a long pause, she concluded, "Either the hollyhocks weren't here, or the boys paid them no mind. If they had stopped to make a beautiful princess, even once, they would not have cut this house in two."

It was mid-afternoon when Coral stood, set her now wilted lady on the step behind her, visited again the living flowers, and walked slowly to her truck. There, she extracted a small notepad and a pencil from the glove box, and with a faraway look in her eyes, wrote a few short phrases on the top sheet. Then she folded the sheet several times, returned to the divided house, and tucked the paper under the siding behind the hollyhocks. After that she drove home, opened all the windows of her house, and sat down to peruse the home furnishings section of the Sears catalogue. Then, ignoring the bank statement that had arrived in the mail in her absence, she drove over to the Church of the Brethren Revitalized and deposited a check in the collection box just inside the double front doors.

Three

Coral Watters was the first, but she was not the only person in Amiable to be singled out for a mysterious unsigned injunction. Over the next few months, several other individuals received the same set of instructions, followed by a different, but equally puzzling, adage. Arlo Blanchard was next.

Tuesday afternoon Arlo was quietly trimming his fingernails on the slightly lopsided front porch of his rectangular red brick home, a structure distinguished by identical chimneys on both ends of the roof. A somewhat muscular man with a growing paunch, a rapidly balding pate, and a graying mustache, he was using a hunting knife for the procedure, which practice invariably led to a verbal exchange with his wife

Perfecting Amiable

Sarah Jean—the same verbal exchange. He always initiated the trimming in front of the TV, and she always said she'd hate for him to cut off a finger or thumb there in the house. In response, he always said okay, he'd cut them off on the porch where she could wash the blood off with the hose. That discussion having already taken place on this occasion, he was on the porch, swinging slowly in the creaky old hanging bench while he worked on his nails. Sarah Jean couldn't let it go, however, and she came to the door and opened the screen. He heard her there and spoke without looking up.

"Who's next?" he said. "Line forms over there for the custom manicure."

"The day I trust you an' that knife with a single finger or toe of mine is the day I go get my head examined," she replied. "Don't expect me to run the movies if you decide to lop off a few of yours."

The Blanchards owned the little rundown theater on Main Street where people came on the weekends unless there was a game of some sort at the high school. Arlo's third-rate films, which arrived by mail every Thursday, could not compete with the excitement of third-rate high school football and basketball, nor with the brawls that typically followed the games. That meant he closed the theater on game nights. His regular job, which in reality was anything but regular, was collecting on overdue bills for the

Marilyn Arnold

Grimm Collection Agency based in Sage, eighty miles up the road. This did not make Arlo a popular man in town, but it did allow him a lot of time to himself because people generally remembered urgent business in the other direction when they saw him approaching.

"You going out to the gypsies today?" Sarah Jean asked. "Maybe you should wait to cut your fingers off until after you've done your business there."

"Yeah, I'm goin' out there. Not that I'll collect anything."

Sarah Jean, a tall, bony woman with uneven teeth and a knobby chin, was referring to the small group of people—squatters, some called them—that had settled more than a year earlier along the bank of the Padre River three miles east of Amiable. No one knew if they held title to the land, or had gotten permission to use it, but everyone assumed they didn't and hadn't. The town merchants willingly sold food and other goods to these people, usually for cash, but occasionally for credit—if they were desperate to unload some piece of merchandise that had been gathering dust for a century or two. Merchants and just about everyone else chose not to associate with them otherwise. Truck drivers made jokes about them, children stared at them, and teenagers mocked them from a distance when they came into town, the men in embroidered tunics and the women in long, broom-pleated skirts.

Perfecting Amiable

Arlo did not have a lot of success with these people when he confronted them about their overdue bills. And since his only pay was a percentage of what he collected, his trips to the squatters were seldom worth the effort. He knew money was scarce over there. A few townspeople bought herbs, and pine nuts, and handmade jewelry from them when they set up a booth in the park. Occasionally, someone would hire one or two of their men to paint a barn or some such. A few of the younger men and women had left the clan and come to live in Amiable. Even they stayed pretty much to themselves, however, and the locals liked to refer to their small social gatherings as "apostate potlucks."

Some assumed the strangers were evangelists, others said they were polygamists or Muslims. Still others insisted they were true gypsies. Arlo didn't care what they were. He had no use for people who didn't pay their bills. Arlo was a man perfectly suited to his job. He rather enjoyed watching people squirm. These people, however, wouldn't squirm. Their philosophy was that if they couldn't pay, they couldn't pay and that was that. When they could, they would. Worrying about it didn't help, so instead they had a party. It drove Arlo crazy. One of the men in particular got Arlo's goat, the apparent leader of the group, Gorah somebody-or-other. Arlo could rant and rave and threaten, but the man remained unruffled.

"I can't give you what I don't have," he would say, smiling. "So relax, and join me for a bit of herb tea."

"I'm tellin' you," Arlo would respond, "you have to pay. They'll throw you in jail, and then where'll you be?"

"In jail, I suppose," Gorah would say, shrugging.

And so Arlo would leave, often as not empty-handed. One of his chief frustrations was that Gorah was not a bad sort, nutty as a fruitcake—but otherwise harmless.

Trying as it was, collecting from the squatters was in reality the least of Arlo's worries. When he and Sarah Jean were on friendlier terms—that is, newly married—they managed to conceive a child, a daughter. Somehow this child went wrong. She fell into drugs and who knows what else. Prostitution, likely, and worse. At sixteen she disappeared one Friday night when Arlo and Sarah Jean were at the movie house. She took some of her clothes and all the money from the top drawer of Sarah Jean's bureau. They never knew where she went or with whom, and they never heard from her again. That was twelve years ago.

The police found no trace of her, and more or less assumed she was gone for good or dead. Arlo and Sarah Jean didn't speak of her any more, but not a day went by that Arlo did not think of her and yearn for her. She evoked the only softness left in the man. He had become crusted over with grief and anger, openly blaming his wife, along with the police, the schools, the Pope, and the president for their loss, and secretly blaming himself. The Blanchards stayed together because they didn't know what else to do, but the warmth

Perfecting Amiable

was gone from their relationship. Arlo found he could be disagreeable without half trying, so he took it up as a kind of alternate career. His anger carried over into his collecting activities, and thus extended also to Gorah and his people.

Arlo had special concerns about the gypsies because he figured they didn't stay in one place very long. They were a roving bunch, and he feared they might skip out before he could collect from them. He voiced his fears to Sarah Jean one night as they stared glumly out at the shadows from the old rockers on their front porch.

"Well, at least you've got the movie house," she said. "We can always live on rancid popcorn, stale jelly beans, and the larder you confiscate from the paying public."

Arlo ignored the comment. He handled operation and maintenance at the theater while Sarah Jean saw to the ordering and returning of films, and oftentimes sold popcorn, candy, and soft drinks. If she wasn't there, the concession stand was closed. The matter was confusing to the patrons because the no-treats-from-outside policy held whether the concession stand was open or not. The whole setup invited cheating, and because folks didn't know until they arrived if the stand would be open for business, many had taken to sneaking candy and cookies into the theater in their pockets and handbags.

Popcorn and drinks were harder to manage, especially in summer when people wouldn't normally wear a coat. So in summer, Arlo required full disclosure from any young person wearing a jacket or carrying a backpack. Some nights he took in enough to provide a week's worth of desserts for the Blanchard household. He also made patrons spit out their gum before entering, but every now and then, somebody slipped by his eagle eye and added yet another wad of gum to the multi-colored collection accruing in the aisles and on the underside of the theater seats.

Arlo was a pain in the neck, but he ran the only movie house in town, so people endured him. In fact, some with deep sorrows of their own cut him a little slack because they knew he still grieved over his lost daughter.

The Blanchards lived in the same house and ate the same food under an informal division of labor contract, but they slept in separate rooms. Still, they found things to talk about when the silence between them grew too heavy. The squatters were a safe topic, and so were the films, the declining quality of popcorn these days, and that odd little Mrs. Ransom who attended neither films nor high school athletic events, but still seemed to know everything about everybody. Rumor had it, too, that she read books, serious books—history, literature, philosophy, and maybe even the Bible—for entertainment, mind you, and not because she had to.

The Carruth brothers were also a favorite topic with Arlo and Sarah Jean because they agreed that the Carruths got what was coming to them for taking a chain saw to a perfectly good

Perfecting Amiable

house, old maybe, but sound. Arlo and Sarah Jean never got to the root of the Carruth trouble, however. Never discussed what led to the splitting of the house. Things like that got too close to home. "What God hath joined together, let not man put asunder," was how Sarah Jean usually ended their discussion on that topic. Arlo never knew whether she was referring only to the Carruth house and the brothers, or whether she also meant the two of them, himself and herself. He never asked for fear she might tell him.

"Them gypsies are gonna slip outta here one day and leave me high and dry," Arlo ventured.

Sarah Jean rocked back and forth a time or two before responding. "What makes you think so? You got your prophet's license?"

Arlo ignored her sarcasm. "I just gotta hunch. You know how they up and appeared that day, outta the clear blue? Well, they could disappear just as quick. Run up some bills and beat it. Shoot, they live in old vans and tents."

"Why do people give 'em credit? It's their own fault."

"They have honest faces. An' they're gentle, you know, kinda sweet. I swear that Gorah fella could talk a bird out of a tree."

Finally, the pair rose wearily from their chairs, methodically turned the cushions over, and shuffled off to their solitary slumbers. At daybreak the next morning, after a fitful night, Arlo grabbed his fishing pole and tackle box—his own, not the library's—from the back screened-in porch and made for his 1990 Ford Bronco. After stowing his gear in the rear of the vehicle, he noticed a folded piece of paper under the windshield wiper on the driver's side. "What's this?" he muttered. "Somebody's idea of a joke, or somebody trying t' sell something?" Arlo was in no mood for a joke, but then he never was. He reached around the windshield post and retrieved the paper. There he read the same set of instructions Coral Watters had received. He was to go to the Carruth house by himself and ponder the so-called maxim written below. He wasn't entirely sure he knew what a maxim was; but when he read what the paper called a maxim, he had a pretty good idea.

In his opinion, though, this one was pure nonsense. He thought such sayings were intended to be full of wisdom. Nothing meant what it was supposed to mean any more. Arlo hadn't opened a dictionary since junior English in high school because it was plain to him that anyone with a grain of intelligence could figure out most words for himself, at least any he needed to know. The rest were superfluous. Even as the word "superfluous" entered his mind, he knew where it came from. Sarah Jean. When it suited her, she threw big words at him to demonstrate what she regarded as the superiority of her intellect and breeding over his. Consequently, she had infiltrated his brain, put words there he had never cared to

Perfecting Amiable

know. Most of the time, however, she forgot herself and talked like ordinary people, which, after all, she was.

It wasn't the word "maxim" that threw Arlo on this occasion. It was what the thing said. There it was, in large, plain capital letters:

WHO BENDS IN NEED FINDS A FRIEND IN DEEDS.

"I'm supposed to ponder this? At the Carruth house? And I'll get some treasure?" Arlo complained. It made no sense to him—not the message, not the instructions—none of it. "It'll be a cold day in Hell b'fore I go over to that dilapidated half-a-house an' ponder anything!"

Arlo decided to get breakfast at the hotel before heading to the river. Hollis Beacham, the proprietor, wasn't in arrears in any of his debts that Arlo knew of and so there wouldn't be any more than the usual unpleasantness between them. Besides, Hollis served an early breakfast for guests on the move. Then, too, sometimes other fishermen started their day with Hollis, and Arlo could overhear conversations about where the fish were biting lately. Today, however, he was distracted. He sat in a corner instead of next to the fishermen's usual table, and when his eggs came he put jam on them instead of on his toast. Then he poured syrup on his potatoes and put salt in his coffee. At last, in disgust, he slammed a few dollars on the table and stomped out. As he left, Hollis called after him, "Nuthin' wrong with them eggs, y' hear? Why're you in such a all-fired huff?"

As he left, Arlo very nearly ran over Mrs. Ransom who was just about to enter the hotel. "My, my," she said, straightening her hat, "aren't we in a hurry this morning?"

"Hmmph. Sorry," Arlo mumbled, bending for the package she had dropped.

He was about to leave when she put her hand on his arm. "I saw you drive past my place yesterday," she said. "I assume you were calling on our transitory friends?"

Arlo frowned. "I had business with them gypsies, if that's what y' mean."

Mrs. Ransom smiled. "They seem like lovely people. So happy and at peace with themselves."

"Well, some a' the rest of us'd be a whole lot happier if them 'lovely people,' as you call 'em, paid their bills. They're parasites, is what they are."

"Oh, come now, Mr. Blanchard, aren't you being a little harsh? What's a few dollars when we can learn so much from people like that, people who have found joy in the simple life?"

"The only thing I've learned from them squatters is how to sponge off your neighbors and the gov'ment."

"Watch their children, how they play together and how

Perfecting Amiable

they respect their parents. Oh, I think we have a good deal to learn from them."

Arlo pulled his arm away. "I gotta go. If I was you, I'd stay away from that crowd. They could rob you some night."

"Oh, I hardly think so. More likely, they would bring me something lovely that they made or found."

"Yeah, found in somebody else's house." Arlo spun around and left Mrs. Ransom shaking her head. Turning back, he saw that she didn't enter the hotel after all, but continued down the street. "Crazy old broad," he muttered.

Arlo drove to the river where he unloaded his fishing tackle and slid down the steep bank to his favorite spot among the willows and rocks. Standing on a large partially submerged boulder, he cast upstream, far out to the middle of the river. Nothing. He cast again. Still nothing. On the third cast, he caught a snag and lost a long length of line and an expensive lure. His mind was not on fishing; his mind was on the message left on his Bronco overnight. "Who bends in need finds a friend in deeds." The words kept running through his mind, and the more he repeated them the more perplexed and angry he became. What business had anybody telling him what to do? Somebody was trying to get his goat, but who? And why? On the next cast, when his line caught on an overhanging branch, Arlo cursed all fish, living or dead, large or small, and packed his gear. This was not his day. Scrambling up the bank, pole in one hand, tackle box in the other, he caught his toe on an exposed root, lost his balance, and fell backwards, twisting his left foot as he went.

Howling with pain, Arlo slid back to the river and gingerly removed his boot. He knew enough to know that a sprain called for ice, and that cold water might help. Perching on a low rock in shallow water, he inched his foot and ankle into the icy river. It was several minutes before he could submerge the tender foot and leave it. As he hunched there, alternately cursing and whimpering, his mind returned to the riddle he was told to solve in order to find a treasure. "What treasure?" he complained aloud. "Nobody said what the fool treasure was. It's prob'ly a joke. Well, I ain't fallin' for it. Not on your life. What kinda fool do they think I am?"

The longer Arlo sat, the more agitated he became. He could see that this thing was going to give him no peace. "Aw right, aw right," he shouted, "I'll do it. I'll go to that half a shack and I'll ponder. But only once. No more." Already Arlo's foot was beginning to swell, and he wasn't sure he could walk to his Bronco, much less climb the steep bank. At least the injury wasn't to his driving foot, and the Bronco had an automatic transmission. "This is a fine kettle of fish," he muttered. "I mean of no fish." His boot was tight on the injured foot, but he was able to get it on if he left the sock off. Arlo pitched his tackle box and pole onto the bank above him and tried to hoist himself up by grabbing roots

Perfecting Amiable

and digging his knees into the loose sod. As he struggled there, strong hands appeared out of nowhere to grasp his elbows and hoist him onto the bank. For a split second, it was not gratitude he felt but annoyance that someone else had invaded his spot. Just his rotten luck, it was Gorah and two boys.

The last thing Arlo wanted was help from the gypsies, but what choice did he have? He thanked them gruffly, pointing to his injured foot, and Gorah introduced his sons, Ilya and Efam. They appeared to be in their early teens, and Arlo could see, in the matter of style, they took after their father. That is, in Arlo's view, they dressed like refugees from the Old Testament. Apparently this bunch had never heard of denims and flannels, the two basic clothing groups among males west of the Mississippi, east of California, and north of Phoenix. The pizza and hamburger of fabrics. The boys' names were almost worse than their attire. If it hadn't been for the pain in his foot, Arlo could not have kept a straight face when he heard the names. Sarah Jean would have said there is nothing like pain to produce good manners in the incorrigible. He wondered where she got words like that, "incorrigible," and she never bothered to tell him, though he suspected her of reading the dictionary when he wasn't around. She would spring them on him when she was losing an argument, and then she would walk off. They were like tape on his mouth. They left him speechless.

Marilyn Arnold

All the way to the Bronco Gorah bragged on his sons—
at least Arlo regarded it as bragging. "Children are such a
joy," he said. "They are my treasure and my pride."

There was that word again, "treasure." Arlo only grunted. He was glad for their help, one boy on each side and
Gorah with the gear, but he didn't want to be beholden. And
he didn't want to hear about anybody's perfect children,
least of all about the offspring of some no-good transient
squatters. As soon as the phrase entered his mind, he knew
Sarah Jean's judgment of it. "Transient squatters," she
would say in a superior tone. "An oxymoron."

"Do you have children?" Gorah asked.

Arlo scowled. "One. A daughter."

"Does she live nearby?"

"No."

"Do you have grandchildren?"

"I don't know."

There was a pause. "Do you know where she is?" Gorah
asked in a kindly voice.

Arlo did not want to have this conversation, not with
anyone, and especially not with this irresponsible intruder.
What business was it of his?

"She left long ago?" Gorah pressed.

"Twelve years," Arlo mumbled. "She could be dead for
all I know. Maybe drugs kilt her." He was grateful to reach the
Bronco. "It's no concern of yours. I c'n manage from here."

Perfecting Amiable

He hesitated, then forced the words out. "Much obliged."

"God go with you," Gorah said, bowing slightly with his hands together in an attitude of prayer.

Arlo's mind was in turmoil as he spun away from the man and his sons and tore down the bumpy dirt road toward the highway. Almost without realizing it, he found himself at the Carruth place, turning in the drive, stopping under the big cottonwood, cutting the engine. He gazed at the house and asked himself why he was here. Then he pulled the message from his shirt pocket and read it again. "Who bends in need finds a friend in deeds." How on earth did that apply to him? Who's bending? What friend? What deeds? His foot hurt, but no more than his heart. In time his foot would heal, but his heart? Perhaps never. A lost child leaves an open wound. He wondered how it was for Sarah Jean, but knew he couldn't ask. She lived in his house, but she had left him, too. Or maybe he had driven her away. A thought struck him full in the face. "What if I'm the one who's lost?" he asked, slowly and deliberately.

At last, the throbbing in Arlo's foot became so severe he had to go home. He needed to elevate the ailing limb. Maybe Sarah Jean would offer to help him with ice packs. Then again, maybe she wouldn't. But maybe he could ask. He was even tempted to show her the paper with the riddle on it, but he could hear her reaction. No, he wouldn't show it to her.

Besides, he was told to keep it to himself. She'd only think his painful foot had made him soft in the head.

When Arlo arrived, Sarah Jean wasn't there, so he had to manage the ice packing himself. It didn't go very well. By the time Sarah Jean returned, he had soaked the sofa where his foot rested, crudely wrapped in a waterlogged dish towel full of melting ice cubes. Her sympathy was not aroused, in all likelihood because her attention had been drawn so powerfully to the wet cushion. To escape her carefully crafted remarks about the mental limitations of a grown man who didn't seem to realize ice melts at room temperature, Arlo hobbled outside, found an old fence pole he could use as a cane, climbed into his Bronco, and started the engine.

Something he couldn't explain propelled him once again toward the Carruth house. He bumped up the driveway at ramming speed, stomped the brake, slid to the passenger side, leaned his back against the door, and stretched his left leg across the seat. As he alternately contemplated the divided house and the unwelcome note, he resented the meddling so-and-so who had destroyed his peace. He also wondered how he was going to do his bill collecting and run the movies with a bum foot.

A week later, Arlo's sprained ankle had improved considerably, though it was still somewhat tender and swollen. In the interim, he had made several unscheduled visits to the

Perfecting Amiable

Carruth house. He didn't know why he went. Maybe it was because he had time on his hands while his ankle healed. In any case, while there he found himself imagining what life must have been like in that household, with enmity festering year in and year out. He realized ill will doesn't sustain itself. It has to be fed. After his third or fourth visit, Arlo came home and actually apologized to Sarah Jean for damaging the sofa. The words nearly choked him, but he managed to get them out. She looked at him quizzically, as if to say, who is this speaking, or am I hearing things? Then she nodded and went back to her knitting.

Arlo cleared his throat and said he guessed that, bad foot or not, it was time for him to pay another visit to the gypsies. Their creditors were leaning on him. Sarah Jean nodded again but said nothing. Arlo dreaded going out there, to where they had set up housekeeping in the long grass and trees. He dreaded it especially because Gorah had learned about Corrie Sue, Arlo's daughter. Arlo still didn't know how he had let that business slip out—but he had. The man asked, and he answered. Clearly he had been in a weakened condition and not himself.

As Arlo pulled up before Gorah's dilapidated van, Gorah stepped out to meet him. "Come, sit here," Gorah said, pointing to a well-worn chair. "I have your money."

"I can't stay," Arlo mumbled, reaching for the envelope in Gorah's hand.

Marilyn Arnold

"I see you're walking, though still with a limp." Gorah said. "Are you healed?"

Arlo thought that an odd way to ask about a foot. He eyed Gorah suspiciously. "Yeah, my foot's a lot better," he said. "Uh, thanks again."

Arlo wanted to open the envelope then and there, to count the money, but his nerve failed him. It would be an insult to the man who had rescued him, so he drove until he was out of sight, then pulled over and opened the envelope. There were a number of bills, mostly twenties and tens, and a note. "Please distribute this money among our creditors, according to their needs," it said. This, instead of a list of creditors and the amount intended for each. That left Arlo with the responsibility of determining who needed the most and who the least. Apparently none of the accounts would be paid in full, at least not yet. Disgusted, Arlo at first didn't notice the postscript at the bottom of the page. Then he saw it. "Go to the fountain in front of the Bellagio in Las Vegas at 3 p.m. Saturday for further healing," it said.

"More riddles!" Arlo yelled, wadding the note into a ball and throwing it to the Bronco's floor to join the clumps of dried mud, the peanut shells, and the empty coke cans. "Is everybody around here batty? My foot's healing fine on its own. I ain't drivin' to no Las Vegas with no sprained ankle—an' that's final!" Besides, he added silently, I've gotta run a movie Saturday.

Perfecting Amiable

Quite to his astonishment, Arlo found himself passing his own street and heading yet again to the Carruth place. A giant magnet it was, relentlessly pulling the Bronco with Arlo inside, unable to resist. This time, he left the Bronco and hobbled up to the house, instinctively trying the back door. It gave. The place was full of the smell of mold and decay. Arlo wondered if that smell sometimes accompanied the death of love. He thought of Sarah Jean and his own home. Had love died there, too? If so, who killed it? He still had said nothing to Sarah Jean about the puzzling message and his covert visits to the Carruth place, but if he was going to Las Vegas, she'd have to know about that. For one thing, she'd have to run the movie. Arlo shook his head in disbelief. Was he actually thinking of driving to Las Vegas on Saturday? What had gotten into him? Was he falling for all this flim flam? If he went, what excuse could he invent? Certainly not one relating to his ankle which, in fact, would argue against the trip.

At home, over supper, which Arlo and Sarah Jean still made the effort to share, Arlo broached the subject. "Looks as if I've maybe gotta go to Vegas Saturday," he mumbled, buttering a piece of bread with studied care.

"Saturday we run a matinee and a night show," she replied.

Arlo cleared his throat and slowly added Smucker's raspberry jam to his bread. "Yeah, I know. Uh, I thought maybe you could handle it this once."

"Well, you thought wrong," she said. "We'll just close the place up so's you can take your little vacation."

"It ain't no vacation. It's business."

"Monkey business, if you ask me."

Arlo didn't know what got into him, but the words came out of his mouth. "You can come along if you want. It ain't a vacation."

Sarah Jean looked at him a long minute. "You serious?" she asked, in a kindlier tone.

"Yeah, sure. We'll close the place up, like you said."

At ten minutes before three that Saturday, Arlo and Sarah Jean Blanchard approached the fountain in front of the Bellagio. Neither had said much on the trip down. She seemed quite relaxed with her book by some dead writer, though she was not particularly friendly, while Arlo was what people call a classic basket case. Sarah Jean knew nothing about Gorah's message, but she had been strangely cooperative about the trip. Arlo figured curiosity had overruled skepticism in his wife, for the moment anyway. And his inviting her to come along proved there was no hanky panky going on. They found a nearby bench in the shade of several decorative trees and, at his insistence, sat down. Sarah Jean's curiosity was aroused.

"What're we doing here, for pity's sake?" she asked. "I hope we didn't drive all the way here to stare at some fountain. We have water at home."

Perfecting Amiable

"I'm just followin' instructions," he replied. "Nobody made you come."

"Whose instructions? What instructions?" she demanded.

"Wait an' see, just you wait an' see. It ain't quite three yet." His eyes were fixed on the fountain and everything around it.

"Well, this is all foolishness, if you ask me. Why, I . . ." Sarah Jean paused, let out a little cry, and rose to her feet. Then she began running, toward a young woman who seemed to be coming toward them.

Arlo rose more slowly, more hesitantly, doubting at first, limping after his wife. Then he knew. "Corrie Sue?" he cried. "Is it you? Corrie Sue!"

That was the moment Arlo's new life began, and Sarah Jean's, too. Driving back to Amiable that night, they talked in the old way, laughing, crying, telling their hopes and fears. In finding their daughter, they also found each other and themselves. How it all happened seemed nothing short of miraculous. They learned that Corrie Sue had spent a few rough years after she left home with a boy they didn't know from Sage. The young pair headed for Las Vegas where they did the drug scene and spent time in jail for petty theft. Corrie Sue never saw him after that. On her release she was afraid to call or come home. Three years ago Gorah and his wife found her hitchhiking south of Henderson, on her way to she didn't know where. Arizona or Mexico. At the time,

Gorah's little band was headed toward the small community of the Havasupai, in a lush green valley up canyon from the Colorado River and the lovely Havasu Falls in western Arizona. The Havasupai had promised to make space and give them work through the tourist season.

Corrie Sue's stay with Gorah's people turned her life around, and when they separated, she had a casino job and a room with friends from work. But Gorah and his wife kept in touch with her, urging her always to make contact with her parents. She had never told them where she was from, or who her parents were. All they knew were the details of her life after she left home. But when Gorah learned about Arlo's missing daughter, he couldn't help wondering. He called her, she confirmed what he hoped, and agreed to a meeting with her parents, on the condition they not be told she would be at the end of their journey. She made it clear that she wanted them to come on faith rather than out of duty. She wanted to see their honest reaction to her, not their prepared response. She was afraid, but she was ready.

When Arlo and Sarah Jean reached their home that night, tired but contented, anticipating Corrie Sue's upcoming visit to Amiable, Arlo told his wife he had one little errand to run before he went to bed. She looked at him questioningly.

"It's all right," he said, patting her hand. "I'll only be a few minutes. Just some unfinished business."

Perfecting Amiable

"We have some of that here, too, so don't dawdle," she said, smiling.

Arlo drove the empty streets to the Carruth house, pulled close to the back entrance, flipped on the Bronco's overhead light, wrote something on a notepad he took from the glove box, then inserted his little composition under the threshold inside the rear door of the house. Then, on a whim, he drove out to the gypsies' encampment by the river before heading home. To his surprise, they were gone. He had wanted to share his joy, but he could see now that Gorah already knew. There was no need for words. A silent farewell to a friend would suffice. "Suffice." Another of Sarah Jean's words.

Four

As far as anyone in Amiable knew, Delsene Parmley had never married. There was that mysterious six-month absence in her early thirties, and people speculated, but she had kept mum on that for a good twenty years now. Which was surprising because it was the only thing she kept mum on. If she had married, or merely run off with some man, it wasn't anybody from around there. People would have known. All they knew for certain was that just prior to her absence, she bought several items from the Amiable Mercantile that were generally purchased by prospective brides. Delicate lingerie, for example, instead of her usual neck-to-toe flannels. When she returned, it was back to flannels. The girls at the Merc swore to it.

Perfecting Amiable

Delsene had ash brown hair which she tinted herself every six weeks. The girls at the Merc said they could set their clocks by it. She had not, however, mastered the art of curling hair, so she left that to the professionals. She lived in a small yellow frame home which her parents willed to her before they died from eating the poisonous wild mushrooms that popped up in their backyard one spring. Delsene had a brother and a sister back East somewhere, or maybe it was California, but no one around Amiable ever saw them any more. Delsene said they weren't the visiting kind, and neither was she. Delsene had a cat, black with white paws, named Mr. Pip, which she adored. Mr. Pip did not return the favor. He was her greatest trial, he and her music students. She taught piano, voice, and violin to Amiable children who were even less gifted than she was.

Delsene had spoiled Mr. Pip so unashamedly that he lost interest in the mice and squirrels she expected him to harvest and thus keep out of her house and apricot tree. He had two bowls on the back steps: one for food and one for water. Delsene always filled both bowls immediately after her own breakfast and before her first lesson. It was summer now, mid-June, so the children were out of school and could take their lessons in the morning. On this particular Monday morning, when Delsene stepped out the back door in her nightgown and hairnet to collect Mr. Pip's bowls, she saw a piece of paper folded under the water bowl. Thinking that odd, since Mr. Pip had never left her notes before, and no one had ever written to him, she bent to pick it up, groaning a bit with her bad hip. She was average in height and slightly stooped, and her aversion to physical exercise had caused her muscles to slide into retirement and her joints to stiffen. She had decided long ago that it was worth the inconvenience. "The only thing I exercise is my prerogative," she liked to say, even though people were so tired of hearing her say it that they didn't bother to laugh politely any more.

The paper under Mr. Pip's bowl contained the same instructions as Coral Watters and Arlo Blanchard had received, but Delsene couldn't read them until she went inside for her glasses, pink-rimmed affairs, that had served her for the last fifteen years. Nothing could have surprised her more than the words she read there, except maybe Mr. Pip's catching a mouse. She should have named him Garfield.

"What's this?" she cried, "a treasure? Where's the map? Listen here to what it says, Mr. Pip." He had just entered the kitchen through his own door, obviously seeking his breakfast. It was the only time he acknowledged that she also lived in his house and was of some limited use to him. She read further. "A riddle? I'm no good at riddles. I need a map. I'm good at maps. I always read the maps on family vacations when I was a little girl. Why, there's nothing I enjoy more to this day than curling up with a good road atlas." At

Perfecting Amiable

one time Delsene had a complete set of USA maps from the AAA, plus Mexico and Canada.

Reading along, Delsene saw the maxim somebody had twisted into a riddle that no one in her right mind could make any sense of:

ALL THAT TITTERS ISN'T TOLD.

She read it to Mr. Pips. "Isn't that the silliest thing? Why would anyone leave such a thing on my doorstep, and under your bowl, Mr. Pip?"

Mr. Pip showed no interest whatsoever. Instead, he padded over to the refrigerator and sat in front of it, like a magistrate before his god. It was the only thing that captured his imagination besides himself. Mechanically, Delsene scraped food from the open can of Fancy Cat cuisine and dumped it into his bowl, failing to notice that she was putting food in the water bowl and water in the food bowl. Mr. Pip would eat and drink from the mixed bowls, but he would not be pleased. Delsene did not notice her error, nor did she notice the unmistakable sneer on Mr. Pip's face as he accompanied her to the back steps.

It was almost time for her first pupil, and Delsene hurriedly dressed in her blue polyester slacks, her pink pullover shirt with a collar, and her white ankle socks with the little black music notes stitched on the sides. It was her teaching uniform. Except on laundry day, or her birthday, her pupils rarely saw her in anything else. Delsene taught piano, voice, and violin because she didn't know what else to do. The town had lacked a piano, voice, and violin teacher, and she stepped up to fill the gap. She got books ordered special from Coral Watters at the library—books on beginning piano, voice, and violin—and followed them religiously, never veering off the prescribed track.

Very few parents seriously questioned her skills, and then only privately, for fear she'd stop teaching and their children would never acquire confidence or be exposed to the higher arts. Every town needed high culture, and Delsene carried that burden for Amiable. More important, she took the children off their parents' hands for an hour or two a week. Delsene never performed at public events, however, pleading always that she had to "save herself" for her students. The townspeople were only too happy to attribute her reticence to modesty and dedication rather than lack of talent. That way they could maintain a comfortable ignorance.

Delsene had known the Carruth boys, of course, and had always resented them just a little—especially before they died—for failing to marry and produce children and grandchildren that she could then instruct in music. Not having a single Carruth child in her home, and thus a direct line to the family's inner sanctums, had been a great trial to Delsene, whose specialty outside of music was "local news," otherwise

Perfecting Amiable

known as gossip. The typical Amiable family produced children with active tongues and no sense of propriety, and thus Delsene was privy to a good share of the doings around town. Even when a child wearied of music lessons, or her parents or his parents did, it wasn't too many years before that child began bearing offspring who were coerced into music lessons as they themselves had been, thereby assuring Delsene continuing access to the family information pipeline.

The trouble was that Delsene was as likely as not to get it wrong when she passed on what she picked up from her pupils. She had a tendency to misunderstand in the first place, and in the second place she had a bad memory for details. But this was no real problem for her because what she didn't actually hear or couldn't remember, she invented. What she could remember she embroidered for her listeners. Delsene had a ready audience for her reports, accurate or not, at the Cuts 'n Curls where she went every week for a shampoo set, and elsewhere, too. Amiable had a little weekly newspaper once, but it couldn't compete with Delsene and folded after a couple of years. Delsene charged nothing for the news she delivered, much less for advertising space, and she was infinitely more entertaining.

Sometimes she erred in not questioning her sources, as when she reported at the beauty salon that the new Bunson baby was not the Bunsons' at all, but had been switched at the hospital in Sage and would have to go back. Her source was six-year-old Benny Bunson, a very serious little boy, a literalist by nature, who had overheard his mother cooing to the baby that he was just too pretty to be theirs and they would have to take him back. Benny arrived at his piano lesson and announced that his parents were sending the baby back. Delsene had no trouble filling in the blanks and adding to the narrative in a way that, in her view, greatly enhanced the story. She had a gift for enlarging and enlivening an otherwise dull set of facts. "I assume the Bunsons will sue the hospital," Delsene had added casually as April rolled a strand of Delsene's hair on a pink plastic curler.

"Y' don't say!" April responded. Y' hear that Miz Dooley?" April addressed the elderly woman in the next chair. "The Bunsons'r suin' the hospital fer switchin' their baby."

Mrs. Dooley, who was hard of hearing, promptly went home and told her husband that the hospital had taken stitches and ruined the Bunsons' baby. The scrambled version of the story was not officially launched until the next day when Mrs. Dooley told what she remembered of it to her sister and niece. By the time the story got back to Delsene, she didn't recognize it and treated it as a new story. The Bunsons were planning to burn the hospital in Sage if its staff didn't stop beating children.

Another time, little Maisie Trenner had arrived for her voice lesson to announce that her father was leaving in the morning.

Perfecting Amiable

"For good?" Delsene had asked, relishing the editorial potential of Maisie's news.

"Uh huh," Maisie answered. "My mama says so."

"Is he coming back?"

"I dunno. My mama says it's good he's going."

Well, that sounded like a split-up to Delsene, and she put Maisie to doing her practice scales while she made a few hurried phone calls. "Yep, she threw him out, as I understand it," Delsene said to her neighbor, Mrs. Stewart. "I'll fill you in later. I've got to run now."

And fill her in she did after Maisie left. By nightfall, thanks to Delsene's ready imagination, the town had the Trenners battered and bruised, with him off to jail and her having changed the locks and engaged an attorney. Delsene was certain, too, that he had another woman somewhere. Of course, the real story was no story at all. Dell Trenner had merely traveled to Clear Springs down the road to repair a water pump, to do what his wife called a good turn, for an aging aunt.

On the day Delsene's mystery message appeared beneath Mr. Pip's food bowl, Delsene just happened to initiate another story. It was all quite innocent, she told herself, because she hadn't intended any harm. When Delsene ushered seven-year-old Kaden Lochtel into her living room for his piano lesson at 9 a.m., his usual time, she was not quite herself. Instead of focusing on Kaden's rendering of "The Pleasant Peasant," her mind kept scurrying off to the note sitting on her kitchen table. She yanked it back, but it refused to stay. When Kaden hit the wrong notes, she patted his head and said "good." When he hit the right notes, she shook her head disapprovingly. Confused, poor Kaden stopped playing and looked at her in dismay.

"But I did good on that part," he complained.

"Oh? uh, so you did. I'm sorry, Kaden. I guess I'm tired. I didn't sleep very well last night. Now, where were we?"

"My daddy slept over to Miss Esplin's last night," Kaden volunteered. Young Miss Esplin lived three houses down from the Lochtels. She taught third grade, and had just moved from the hotel to her own little house.

"Huh? What's that?" Delsene heard that remark, all right. Her brain went on auto-pilot and registered such things even when nothing else stuck. She could feel it kick into high gear as it processed Kaden's report. Satisfied with what it regarded as the essentials, her brain closed up like an evening primrose at noon and completely blocked his next comment.

"Miss Esplin went to Sage. Her lock's broke," Kaden said, but his words fell on deaf ears.

As it happened, Mondays were Delsene's shampoo set days, and it was a trial of patience for her to get through her morning music lessons. Once she reached the Cuts 'n Curls,

Perfecting Amiable

however, she was well rewarded for her suffering. Every chair was full, including those provided for spectators. In a small town like Amiable, sometimes a woman's chief afternoon entertainment was moseying on down to the local beauty salon to watch the comb-outs and hear the latest gossip. This particular Monday was a red letter day, indeed, for news bearer and audience alike. With no little effort, Delsene muzzled her news bulletin until she surfaced from the shampoo. She wanted eye contact when she delivered this little bombshell, and she wanted to see the effects of the flying shrapnel. It was her proudest moment.

She looked around, cleared her throat loudly, and waited for the silence she knew would ensue when it became clear that she had news. "Hank Lochtel is having an affair with Miss Lisa Lorraine Esplin!" Delsene announced at last, her chin thrust high. "I have it on the best authority."

Initially, there was shock all around—which Delsene noted with obvious satisfaction—and a mild protest from a few, which she ignored. Hank Lochtel was reputed to be a devoted husband and father. Why, he even took vacations with his family, the ultimate proof. And it was rumored that he read to his children at bedtime, though that rumor hadn't been confirmed by unbiased authority. Of course, the fall of such paragons of virtue is more gratifying to the flawed onlooker than the fall of someone with a more shadowy reputation. That being the case, the doubters came around quickly and joined wholeheartedly in the feast.

"Why, I wouldn't have believed it for a minute, if it hadn't come from your very lips," Elsa Prosser said from under the hair dryer. "Imagine that, Hank Lochtel. I feel sorry for the children, is who I feel sorry for."

"I always thought it suspicious, that cute little school marm moving into that there house so close to the Lochtels," Vonda Richey chimed in from a spectator chair.

"I ain't the least bit surprised, m'self," Beryl Everly said from the chair where she was being permed. "I hear that wife a' his is a real nag."

"Yeah," Vonda observed, "she musta been potty trained at gunpoint."

Delsene looked about at her cohorts. She knew the news would be all over town by nightfall, and that she was the genius behind it. They would give her credit, most of them anyway. She smiled and nodded at each comment, every now and then adding to the growing body of assumptions and surmises. Say what you want about the speed and convenience of the internet, it can't touch the small town information highway for coverage and inaccuracy. In its sphere, the latter is without parallel.

Delsene went to bed happy that night, knowing she had served her community well and solidified her position among the women at the Cuts 'n Curls. She even temporarily forgot

Perfecting Amiable

the note she had found that morning. The trouble began three days later when the Wallabees returned from a brief trip to Grand Junction. On the way, the Wallabees had stopped over for supper in Sage. And who should they have seen there but Miss Esplin, taking a late supper with her sister—on the very night Hank Lochtel stayed in Miss Esplin's home. As it turned out, Hank's wife had volunteered his "watch dog" services so that Miss Esplin would not worry over leaving her house unprotected in her absence. In the meantime, Miss Esplin had gone to her sister's for a visit and would return when Mr. Hassler, the local handyman, got her lock fixed or replaced. Kaden Lochtel had said as much, but it had not registered in Delsene's busy brain.

This time Delsene had made an error that could seriously affect her standing in Amiable. A few women who had helped spread the story still clung to the hope that Delsene was right about Hank. After all, he had stayed in Miss Esplin's house, hadn't he, regardless of what anybody said? That much was undisputed. Most, however, were as ready to denounce Delsene as they had been to admire her. Some went so far as to cancel music lessons for their children. In her darkest hour Thursday evening, Delsene remembered the mystery note. She removed it from the large recipe box where she had put it for safe keeping, along with her living will, several coupons for plug-in air fresheners, six credit card applications from

Marilyn Arnold

Wells Fargo, and her cooking hairnet. There were no recipes in the box; any she had saved from her mother or clipped from *Woman's Day* were loose in the drawer beneath the breadbox. Occasionally Delsene shuffled through the recipes, but usually gave up the search in favor of a ready-prepared Lean Cuisine meal or a Totino's pizza from her freezer.

Delsene retrieved her eyeglasses from atop the refrigerator, spread the note across the kitchen table, and read it again. In concentrating her attention on the promise of treasure and the question of a map, she had more or less forgotten—or repressed—the part about going to the Carruth house and pondering. She couldn't remember pondering at any time in her life, though she came close when her parents ate those mushrooms and died so fast. In Delsene's world, you got information and you passed it on as quickly as possible to deserving friends and neighbors. Information was not to be hoarded like vanilla from Mexico or chocolate from Switzerland. That was Delsene's standard operating procedure, and generally, she thought, it had served her well. She still saw herself as a person of considerable influence in Amiable. If it got out that she was pondering on a given day, and worse still, doing it at the old Carruth house, why she might as well turn in her badge and leave. People around here didn't understand that kind of behavior. Add that to the Lochtel gossip that went sour on her, and you've got trouble right here in River City.

Perfecting Amiable

Once more, Delsene read the cryptic message that she was to ponder: "All that titters isn't told." Again, she failed to see the connection to herself. "Well!" she exclaimed, "I might's well sneak out there to the Carruth place. I don't see what good it'll do, but I couldn't be any more in the dark than I am now. Or have more time on my hands."

Sitting there in the fading light, staring at the divided house from the open window of her 1994 Honda Civic, trying to do whatever it was the note called pondering, Delsene Parmley was completely befuddled. She couldn't seem to get into the spirit of the game, if indeed a game is what it was. Did the note carry just the slightest hint of criticism, the slightest suggestion that she was not perfect just as she was? No, she dismissed that thought. What on earth did she need to change? She couldn't see it.

"Now the Carruth boys," she said aloud, "there were two fellas who needed to change and everybody could see it. Look at that house. What a sad mess. It would have broken their poor parents' hearts. Prob'ly did, newly arrived in heaven and not used to the change yet either. But what's it got to do with me?"

Delsene made a quick U-turn in the yard and drove back to the highway. There, off to the side of the road, was some kind of older car, she couldn't tell what. She was tempted to drive on by, but someone was standing in front of it, waving her down. In this town you couldn't ignore a call for help even if you wanted to. Everybody would know. At times like this, Delsene could see that living in a big city had its advantages. In a city you could even ignore a murder in progress under your very nose, not to mention somebody with car trouble. The person waving at her, Delsene saw now, was Mrs. Ransom. Most people regarded the older woman as harmless, though some thought her too liberal in her thinking for a town like Amiable. Why, she had even been friendly with the gypsies. And she was pleasant all the time and never spoke ill of anyone. Delsene found it hard to trust someone who smiled a lot. That person was likely to have something up her sleeve.

But here Delsene was, obligated to stop because not everybody in town had the foresight and intelligence to drive a reliable automobile like a Honda Civic. "Car trouble, Mrs Ransom?" she called in a friendly voice even though she was in no mood to be friendly.

"Yes, dear," the older woman replied. "I'm so glad you came by. Could you take me home, perchance? I can have George at the Texaco pick up my car in the morning. Perhaps it's merely out of gas."

Delsene hesitated. "Well, I am in something of a hurry," she said, "but I suppose . . ." She didn't relish driving with Mrs. Ransom, who was sure to have heard of her blunder with the Lochtel story. The woman's twinkly eyes had a way of seeing into your soul. Delsene didn't trust her as far as she

Perfecting Amiable

could throw her, which, despite the woman's diminutive frame, wasn't very far.

"Oh, are you dear? Well, perhaps I can catch someone else, though it is growing rather late."

Delsene was trapped. She couldn't leave Mrs. Ransom out here by herself in the dark. "Yes, it is. You'd better hop in. I'll take you home."

"I do so hate to be a nuisance," Mrs. Ransom apologized as she pushed aside the note on the front seat.

Delsene snatched the note and put it on her own lap, then spun onto the highway. She was determined not to look at Mrs. Ransom and, if possible, to drive out to the woman's house without engaging in conversation. She saw at once, however, that it was not possible. Worse still, Mrs. Ransom was not a woman who minced words.

"I see you had occasion to visit the Carruth house," she ventured.

Delsene didn't respond.

"Do you know, the story of those brothers was the first story I heard when I moved to Amiable." She paused. "It seemed everybody couldn't wait to tell me, as though they took some kind of pride in it." She paused again. "I'm quite sure, too, that the story and the brothers have suffered in the retelling, aren't you?"

Delsene was in a corner. She had to answer. "I s'pose."

"I always remember what Jesus taught on the subject,"

Mrs. Ransom said. "You recall that he said it wasn't what went into the mouth that defiled a man, but what came out of it." She paused. "He was talking about words."

Delsene was not comfortable with this conversation, so she reached forward and turned on the radio. Some call-in talk show was on the air, and someone was ranting against nutty environmentalists who were trying to preserve the planet at the expense of people who had a god-given constitutional right to drive gas guzzlers if they wanted, and pollute rivers if they wanted, and kill rare birds, and cut rain forests and so on.

Mrs. Ransom looked over at Delsene and smiled, her signal that she recognized the conversation was over.

Delsene did not have what you would call a tranquil night. Moreover, she forgot to fill Mr. Pip's water bowl before she went to bed. In retribution, he scratched a hole in the side of her almost new (four years old) sofa before setting up a clam-or at her bedside. Even so, Mr. Pip's antics were the least of her worries. It was Mrs. Ransom that unnerved her. If she had ever heard the words of Jesus that Mrs. Ransom quoted, she had either forgotten them or assigned them some harmless meaning. But now she couldn't get them out of her head. She always thought of herself as Christian, though she wasn't what you'd call active in any one brand of it. She worshiped with the Methodists at Christmas and the Catholics at Easter, and once or twice a year she attended Relief Society socials

Perfecting Amiable

with a couple of Mormon women who sent their children to take music lessons with her. She consciously stayed away from the Church of the Brethren Revitalized because she thought them a little too southern for her taste.

The next morning—Delsene was free because she had cancellations of her scheduled lessons—she decided to return to the Carruth house and think things through. This was a new experience for her, thinking things through, and she had no natural aptitude for it. Oh sure, she talked to Mr. Pip on occasion, but generally about nothing more serious than whether or not she should subscribe to satellite television on her limited income. Of course, she would remind him, she had a small monthly stipend from her parents' trust, but she hated to tap into that for luxuries. No matter, at 9 a.m. she found herself once again turning into the driveway of the divided house. She noted that Mrs. Ransom's car was gone and credited George with its removal.

The message left under Mr. Pip's bowl was there on the dashboard where she had put it after delivering Mrs. Ransom home last night. Delsene pulled around the back and parked as close as she could get to the rear door of the Carruth house. The last thing she wanted was to be seen here, especially in the morning, when everyone supposed she was fully scheduled for music lessons now that it was summer. Most of all, she did not want to be seen here again by that smiling busy-

Marilyn Arnold

body, Mrs. Ransom. The woman had a way of unnerving a person; Delsene was certain she did it on purpose, and that she enjoyed it. Satisfied that she couldn't easily be seen from the road, Delsene smoothed the paper and read it all again, from start to finish. Her mind came to rest on the adage that had been remodeled until it was incomprehensible: "All that titters isn't told."

"What happened to gold and glitter?" she asked out loud. "How long can a person of sound mind and body ponder five words—six, if you count 'isn't' as two—and most of them not full-sized words, either, but little bitty words?"

She opened the car door to get some air. As she looked across the unkempt yard, Delsene noticed that some of the large dandelions that had more or less taken over the grass plot behind the house had already gone to seed. "Too bad what's happened to this place since the Carruth boys got themselves killed," she said, stepping to the ground and absently plucking a green stem with a delicate ball of feathery seeds on the end of it. Then on an impulse, Delsene became a child again, taking a deep breath and blowing the seeds to kingdom come. She smiled to see them take flight, become tiny paratroopers floating slowly to earth, their parachutes above them, shiny disks in the sun. Then the thought came to her: Could a person gather in that myriad of flying seeds and attach them once more to that single dandelion stem? She answered her own question. Of course not.

Perfecting Amiable

At that moment a breeze swirled from behind her and caught the chutists, lifting them, spreading them, carrying them to some unknown destiny. As if in response, a song sparrow on a nearby shrub lent his music to their flight. Delsene caught her breath. It was the first time she had noticed a bird song in years, or blown a dandelion. Then it hit her, and the words Mrs. Ransom had quoted came back—not what goes into the mouth, but what comes out of it, that's what defiles. The breath that launched the dandelion seeds is the same breath that launches words, and words sent out cannot be retrieved any more than seeds caught in the wind or the song of a bird sent forth.

"All that titters isn't told, or shouldn't be," Delsene declared slowly as she walked to the back step of the Carruth house and sat heavily. She didn't even bother to remove a tissue from her pocket and wipe the step first. Sitting there, she couldn't help wondering about the words that might have flown about that unhappy house. By the time she arose some forty minutes later, Delsene knew what she had to do. She went to her car, found a pencil, and scribbled something about dandelions on a piece of paper. Tucking the paper under the nearest window frame, Delsene walked to her car and drove home. When she entered the back door, she could have sworn that Mr. Pip appeared pleased to see her. It was a first.

Five

Tyrel Fernley was only thirty-two years old and had lived in Amiable just four years, but already he had earned the resentment of about everybody in town who could spell the word without looking it up. Orphaned at the age of sixteen, he was one of those unbridled born-again evangelists, but that wasn't what turned people against him the most. What turned them against him the most was that he had won every raffle anybody sponsored ever since he moved to Amiable. You name it, he won it, whether it was a turkey from the Rotary Club, or five free car washes at the Gas and Go, or a bag of seed corn at the Amiable Mercantile—he won it. Not that he had any use for much of the stuff he won, except

Perfecting Amiable

maybe those imported gold fish and a year's supply of gold fish food from the Ladies League. Even then, he had to buy a bowl for the fish, and people said they bet he never cleaned it. They gave the fish a week to live, at most.

It was getting so businesses and churches and civic clubs were reluctant to hold raffles any more, for fear nobody else would buy raffle tickets if they knew Tyrel had bought one. And he never kept the fact of his purchase to himself, but broadcast it all over town. Sponsors of such events didn't dare refuse him a ticket because what if he up and sued them for discrimination? One by one, however, these organizations turned away from raffles and toward auctions for fundraising because Tyrel did not have a whole lot of cash, and that gave others a chance to win. But it also took away some of the fun because there weren't a whole lot of people in Amiable with money to spend on the pleasure of outbidding each other. Therefore, the few who had spare cash dominated the action at such events, unless some poor soul like Martel Jones got carried away and bid next month's mortgage payment to get a fancy doghouse and then had to sleep in it until his wife forgave him. In the heat of the moment, he completely forgot that they didn't have a dog because his wife was allergic to all things canine.

Even with Tyrel's uncanny luck, it wouldn't have been so bad if he'd been even a little humble about winning, and had acted even the tiniest bit surprised when his name was called.

But he always acted as if it was a foregone conclusion, and people were beginning to think it was. Some went so far as to suspect fraud. Maybe the worst part of it was that Tyrel gave God the credit for his luck in the raffles, as if the Lord took even the slightest interest in who got the Thanksgiving turkey in Amiable, Utah. Moreover, everyone said, if he did take interest, Tyrel would be the last person he would choose. Instead of Tyrel, he would choose someone poor with a big family, someone who needed a turkey. He would not choose someone who was puffed up and wouldn't know how to cook a turkey if his life depended on it. But Tyrel always said the Lord was rewarding him, Tyrel Fernley, his chosen servant, for his righteousness.

The last raffle held in Amiable was sponsored on Memorial Day, a year earlier, by the Daughters of the American West, which was the name the Ladies League adopted for special occasions. For that crowning event, the Merc had donated a hand-push lawn mower to the Daughters. Never mind that it had been gathering dust for several years because everybody who could afford it used a power mower these days, or just brought in the goats. The women were trying to raise money to install a new flag pole and flag in front of the elementary school. People thought sure Tyrel would not buy a raffle ticket for a lawn mower because he had no lawn. But that didn't stop him. Naturally, he won, and there the lawn

Perfecting Amiable

mower sat, turning orange with rust next to his sorry-looking house trailer which could not, by any stretch of the imagination, be called a mobile home.

The three of them are there together, trailer and lawn mower and Tyrel, in an abandoned RV park on the west edge of town. Somehow he figured out how to tap into the water and electric lines that used to service the whole park, and nobody reported him. Townsfolk admired the utilities people even less than they admired Tyrel Fernley and were rather pleased to see a heartless company snookered by so simple a soul as Tyrel. But there was one thing people didn't understand: they didn't understand why Tyrel spent a good portion of his days in front of an antiquated computer playing the stock market. If appearances were any indication, Tyrel hadn't struck it rich yet and probably never would.

The fact that thus far in his life riches had eluded him was a total mystery to Tyrel. He couldn't figure out why there had been no divine intervention on his behalf in the stock market, as there clearly had been in the raffles. After puzzling over the matter for some time, Tyrel concluded that the Lord was merely testing him and by and by his meager investments would turn big profits. Indeed, this was the subject of many a pious prayer sent skyward from his house trailer. Beyond that, he even sought to parley with Jesus on the internet, trying a variety of online addresses—heaven, Kolob, cloud nine, Jerusalem, Zion, the Vatican, Salt Lake

City—but got no reply he regarded as genuine. Oh, he got responses all right, mostly from California, Arkansas, Texas, and Florida; and he was surprised at the number of self-proclaimed Messiahs doing business on Yahoo.

While a lesser man would have become discouraged and abandoned the quest, Tyrel persisted. Ultimately, his persistence was rewarded. In fact, Tyrel's real life, as he believed, began when a heaven-sent manifestation revealed to him that he was, in very fact, the anointed prophet of the one true church of Divine Capitalism. That revelation came to him in the middle of the night, when he left his bed to get a glass of purloined water. He walked barefooted to the doorway of his trailer house and stepped out onto the rickety metal step that was attached to the trailer by two bent screws, both of them loose. At the precise moment Tyrel stepped out, the screws gave one last protest and let go, sending Tyrel plunging to the ground head first.

The fall knocked him out cold, and when he came to, he knew the bump on his head was a sign that he had been called. As he staggered to his feet, Tyrel saw by the moonlight that the glass he was carrying had broken and bloodied his right hand. Leaning against the trailer, he stared at his hand, then solemnly touched it to his forehead, as a sign that he accepted the call. It was like Isaiah's burning coal. He would found a church, and salvation through capital investment would be its motto and its watch cry. Tyrel had tried just about every

Perfecting Amiable

known church on the planet in his thirty-two years, and he had never found the right fit. So of late, he had more or less followed the course of a saintly independent, a course which he could conveniently design himself. Now he would take up his true calling; he would be a prophet-preacher. He had always suspected that he had a gift for preaching, and now he was convinced that there was both salvation and money to be made in preaching speculation.

"I have been called," Tyrel announced to the lawn mower. "I will begin my ministry in the town of Amiable. These here people've already seen the hand of a beneficent deity in my life. Ain't the raffles proof?"

Tyrel envisioned a great future for himself as he gazed at the night sky and wiped his bloody hand on his pant leg. Once sufficiently grounded in the principles he was to teach, he saw himself taking to the road, preaching to large gatherings of adoring (and affluent) followers. From there the next step might be talk radio. The possibilities, he could see, were endless. After all, who in this day and age wouldn't be glad to hear that Jesus invented money and the stock market? Nobody was teaching that doctrine that he knew of. He would be the first and the greatest, though surely giants would follow in his footsteps. He would be honored and revered. It brought tears to Tyrel's eyes to consider it. He, Tyrel Fernley, had been chosen to spread near and far the message of salvation through wealth. Thousands would flock to him and seek to worship at his feet, but he would modestly collect his fee and give the credit to Jesus.

The next day, while his head still throbbed as a poignant reminder of his call, Tyrel prepared notices to post on utility poles, fences, and vacant store fronts around town. The text of his hand-printed notices (Tyrel had no printer for his recycled computer) read:

JESUS WANTS YOU TO BE RICH!!!
HE HAS REVEELED THIS TO HIS CHOZEN SERVUNT
WHO WILL TEACH THIS NEW ADVANCED GOSPIL.
GATHER WITH THE CHOZEN FAITHFUL AT CENTRAL
PARK PAVILYUN
JULY 10 AT 6 P.M.

Tyrel would have added the phrase "of Divine Capitalism" to the third line, but he wasn't sure how to spell "capitalism." Besides, he wanted to surprise people. He set the gathering three days in advance so he could nail down the principles he wanted to teach and figure out how best to assure this event and other activities would compensate him adequately for his inspired service to humanity. It even crossed his mind that he might apply to some benevolent foundation for a grant so he could devote full time to the ministry. He overheard Coral Watters tell the girls in the Merc that she planned to apply for a grant to install a temperature control system in the library—for the comfort of

Perfecting Amiable

both the books and herself—so he knew such things were available for worthy causes. He could think of no cause worthier than his own financial security into infinity.

Armed with hammer, tacks, and flyers, Tyrel issued forth from his house trailer on the bicycle he had won the previous September in a raffle in Clear Springs. (Before riding away with the prize, he had been enjoined by the mayor to confine his blankety-blank raffle activities to his own town.) As it happened, the Carruth house stood between Tyrel's "homestead" and the main part of Amiable. That meant he had to pass the halved structure on his way into town. On an impulse, Tyrel pedaled up the now somewhat overgrown Carruth driveway. He was surprised to see evidence that vehicles had been in the drive of late, dripping oil and squashing weeds. Leaning his bicycle against the exposed front wall of the house, he nailed a flyer to the nearest corner. It crossed his mind that he might consider moving his trailer house here and squatting on this property instead of where he was. The trees were nicer here, too, and it was a little closer in. He wondered why no one had thought of it before, but then he realized that most people are not as resourceful as he himself. Nor had they the intellectual gifts of the sanctified.

As with just about any diversion in a small town, people are so glad for something out of the ordinary to happen that Tyrel's activities attracted more than a little attention in Amiable. Youngsters with nothing to do until their little league games that evening began collecting in his wake as he tacked announcements on just about anything unoccupied that would take a nail, including signs reading "Post no Bills."

"Hunh. Post no bills," Tyrel read. "Now, who on earth's gonna do that? A bill comes for somethin' you bought. You pay it, you don't tack it on a pole!" He snorted at the thought. "On the other hand, maybe they meant money," he said. "But who in his right mind's gonna tack real money to an ol' pole or fence?"

Tyrel solved the problem by covering the ridiculous signs with his own notices wherever he could. At least his notices made sense. Once that job was done, he headed back to his trailer where, with the help of heaven-sent enlightenment, he intended to clarify in his own mind what was meant by the Gospel of Divine Capitalism.

Tyrel loved the term "Divine Capitalism," more especially because he invented it, and he vowed to preach whatever it was. He settled into his favorite army surplus camp chair, which sat in the middle of his box on wheels because that's the only place there was room for it. There, with the Bible on one knee and a notepad on the other, Tyrel was poised to receive knowledge from above. He squeezed his eyes tight, opened and closed his mouth several times to clear his cranial cavity, and shouted, "Amen, Jesus, gimme the words!" Nothing happened. He tried again. Still nothing. Perplexed,

Perfecting Amiable

he walked to the door and stepped down onto an old crate somebody had left at the RV site, the crate now serving as his front step. There, Tyrel tipped his head back, raised both arms to the sky, and shouted again, "Amen, Jesus, gimme the words!" Again nothing. "Time's a wastin', Lord," he said after several minutes. "I on'y got 'til Saturday, y' know."

Apparently Jesus did know because he took time from his other labors to come and tip that wobbly crate over. Once again Tyrel tumbled at his own door step, though with less bodily injury on this occasion. As he landed on his left hip and elbow, the Bible flew out of his grasp. Moaning, he crawled over to where the Good Book lay open in front of him. Closer inspection revealed that the exposed pages included most of Matthew 25. There before Tyrel's eyes were the parable of the ten virgins and the parable of the talents. He took that as a clear sign from on high and scrambled back to his thinking chair. Satisfied that the parable about twelve young women short on oil couldn't be intended for him, Tyrel went to work on the parable of the talents. He read and re-read it, scratching his head where the bump wasn't. Then revelation struck. "Saints be praised!" he hollered. "Here in plain sight fer them as has ears t' hear is the Gospel of Divine Capitalism, an' Jesus his own self is preachin' it!" Tyrel was ecstatic.

Saturday was rather cloudy and the air held the delicious promise of rain, but a large crowd turned out at the park pavilion, anyway. There had been a good deal of speculation at the Merc and at Sally's Saloon and Grill, not to mention the Cuts 'n Curls, as to what that no-good fanatic of a raffle winner was up to. Amiable's mayor, Dorsen Ruckles, in a show of authority, even wore a suit. A good many dogs turned out, too, but the cats all stayed home, which disputes the old adage about cats and curiosity because cats aren't nearly as curious as dogs and people when it comes to extemporaneous revival meetings. That local cats boycotted the event also witnesses to the greater intelligence of cats. It is probably safe to say it was not a religious impulse that brought most of Tyrel Fernley's congregation to the park. In fairness, however, it must be admitted that a few honest seekers were scattered among the curious and the corruptible.

At the appointed hour, the mayor stepped forward as though to conduct the meeting, which was, after all, on public property; but Tyrel beat him to it. He leaped to the pavilion platform in a navy blue, three-piece suit that was clearly two or more sizes too large. The cuffs were frayed, the seat was shiny, and Tyrel smelled of mothballs. No one had ever seen the suit before, on or off its current occupant.

Hollis Beacham, the hotel proprietor, turned to Feston Hassler, the local handyman. "Where d' you s'pose he got that suit?" Hollis asked.

"Mos' likely from the dump!" Feston replied with a chortle. "I'd hide in the cellar 'fore I'd come out in sump'n looked that bad. Or wear a sack on m' head!"

"Hey, Tyrel," Hollis shouted out, "is that yer official preacher's suit, or are them yer pajamas?"

Everybody laughed.

"You c'n laugh now," Tyrel responded, addressing the gathering, "but one a' these days you'll be cryin' if'n you don't listen up to what I got t' say." He ignored the murmuring and went on. "I'm here t' tell you how t' get rich Jesus' way. I'm here t' tell you he wants you t' be rich!"

"Then we're on the same page because that's what I want, too," offered Emmarene Woolsey, who taught fifth graders at the Amiable Elementary School. "All you have to do is look at Tyrel and you know Jesus has made him wealthy. We should all be so lucky."

The people around her laughed.

"Oh, ye of little faith!" Tyrel cried. "Listen up t' what's right here in holy writ. You c'n go home and read it in the twenty-fifth chapter of Saint Matthew. Right outta the mouth a' Jesus hisself. I ain't lyin'. The parable a' the talents. Right here in black an' white Jesus says to invest yer money. A 'talent,' y' see, is a Bible word fer money. Now, they din't have no stock market in Jesus' day, but the principle's the same. Today we got the stock market an' I'm prepared, because I been called, t' invest fer you whatever moneys you want t' see grow. That man in the parable what took two talents an' invested them to make four, his boss says good fer you and give him more. That other man what took five talents an' invested them t' make ten, his boss says good fer you, too, and give him more." Tyrel paused and lowered his voice. "But how about that fella what took his one talent an' buried it fer fear a' losin' it? Why, his boss chews him out good and takes away the one measle talent he had."

Tyrel stopped and looked a number of people in the eye. "An' that, my friends," he announced with an air of finality, "is the Gospel of Divine Capitalism, in a nutshell. Straight outta the holy book, straight outta Jesus' own mouth." A few, including Coral Watters and the Blanchards and Delsene Parmley, shook their heads and left. Mrs. Ransom stood off to the side, a bemused smile on her face.

"Don't leave, folks. I'm startin' up a church based on that there holy principle," Tyrel cried. "Anybody wantin' to join up can do so fer the measle sum of ten dollars. I'll pass around this here Poppycock popcorn can with a pencil and notepad. Put yer membership fee in the can and yer name on the notepad. That's all there is to it. Easier'n fallin' off a log."

The "take" from Tyrel's revival meeting did not appear to be impressive, nor was the length of the membership list when the notepad came back. He noted that somebody tried to be cute and signed up his dog and horse. Disappointed but not defeated, Tyrel put his Bible and notepad in the basket attached above the rear fender of his bicycle and headed home

Perfecting Amiable

to regroup. By the time he arrived at the RV park, he felt a little better, a little more optimistic. In his heart he knew that all the great prophets suffered setbacks. "Jesus hisself din't have no easy go of it," he said aloud. "Why, they even kilt him!"

Inside the house trailer, Tyrel tossed his Bible and notepad onto the small table that served as computer desk and eating surface, often at the same time. As he did so, a paper folded several times flew out of the notepad. "Ah," he said, "somebody too shy t' join with the faithful in public worship wants his name—or it could be a her—registered among the saints." The contents of the note, however, completely baffled him. He didn't know it, of course, but the instructions he received were the same as those for the earlier recipients of a similar missive. What was different was the riddle. When he read it, the thing sounded like some of the sayings his mother used to recite, by way of instruction, only hers made sense and this didn't. As he read the statement, Tyrel had to laugh. Who had the gall to tell him, a chosen prophet, to spend his precious time and energy pondering some nutty saying, and at the Carruth house, no less! "The place is prob'ly infested with all kinds a' vermin," Tyrel said. But his eyes kept returning to the ridiculous saying, printed in large capital letters near the bottom of the page:

ABSURD TO THE WISE IS DEFICIENT.

Marilyn Arnold

Tyrel read the thing again and again, out loud, but could see no application whatsoever to himself. Either this note was misplaced or somebody was making a bad joke. "I ain't goin' over to no tattered ghost house and ponder nuthin'!" he declared. "Besides, how c'n I ponder when I got a church to organize and run?" Pranksters who wrote notes like that didn't realize what a burden they put on hard-working, conscientious people like himself. For example, Tyrel had not even counted the money he took in for memberships today; that's how distracted he was. Scanning his one-room house trailer and seeing no trace of the Poppycock popcorn can he had circulated at the meeting, Tyrel concluded that he must have left it in his bicycle basket. Carefully lowering himself onto the repositioned crate he used for a step, Tyrel rummaged through the basket. No can. He panicked. Where could it be? Did he leave it at the pavilion, or did it bounce out of his bicycle basket on the way home?

No time to waste, Tyrel thought as he hopped on his bicycle and headed back to town. His mind turning faster than his feet, Tyrel raced toward the park pavilion near the center of town. As he entered an intersection near the park, he failed to notice both the stop sign on his right and the faded maroon Chevy Cavalier coming from his left. The Chevy didn't hit him, he hit the Chevy, broadside. He felt himself sailing through the air and landing in a heap. "I've got t' quit fallin' down, though I'm partial t' flying," he said

Perfecting Amiable

before he lost consciousness.

The next thing Tyrel knew, the delicate smell of lilac pierced his consciousness. A woman's voice was saying, "Are you all right? Are you all right? I didn't see you coming. You ran right into me!"

A male voice broke in. "That's right, lady, he rode right into you. I seen it all. Hope you've got insurance 'cause I bet he don't."

"We'd better call the ambulance."

Tyrel did not want the ambulance. He wanted his Poppycock can. "No . . . no ambulance," he stammered. "Gotta find Poppycock . . . gotta find money."

"What's that he's sayin'? Poppycock? Money? He's outta his head. Better get 'im to the clinic pronto."

"No . . . no clinic," Tyrel protested. "Park. Pronto. Poppycock."

"Why's he keep on sayin' Poppycock?" the male voice asked. "Izzy hungry?"

"I don't think so," the female voice said. "I wonder if he's broken anything."

"Broken commandments," Tyrel mumbled. "No broken commandments."

As it turned out, Tyrel broke his bicycle and his left arm in his broadside crash into a car and subsequent free-form flight across Oak Street. He also acquired another bump on his head. The owner of the Cavalier was Brionna Lee Wells, who worked the graveyard shift at Sally's Saloon and Grill, the only all night café and truck stop in town. Everyone knew that two years ago Brionna Lee had delivered a baby boy out of wedlock, and that the father of the child had deserted long before the birth. Brionna kept the baby, though, and worked nights so she could be with him during the day. The two of them were living with her parents until she could buy a little place of her own. She was running to the Merc for groceries when Tyrel slammed into her. Luckily, her little boy was at home.

With the help of a gentleman who witnessed the mishap, a visiting cousin of Eddie Gertz, Brionna Lee managed to get Tyrel into the back seat of the Cavalier and over to the clinic. She insisted over his protests, and all the way to the clinic he mourned his lost Poppycock can. Brionna waited with him while Doctor Hooper checked his head and made repairs on his skinned knees, hip, and fractured left arm. Then she took him and his mangled bicycle home. Doctor Hooper was the only certified physician in town, though Amiable was blessed with two good nurses, one or two quacks, and a fellow who had taken a three-week course in acupuncture. So far, the latter had punctured numberless blood vessels, two lungs, and one pace maker. Business in the emergency life flight industry picked up considerably after he arrived.

Perfecting Amiable

Late that afternoon, Tyrel concluded that he was apparently going to live, so he arose stiffly from the lumpy mattress that served him as a sofa during the day and a bed at night. The mattress lay on a built-in frame at one end of the trailer. The kitchen area and tiny bathroom were at the opposite end. Tyrel could not remember when he had cleaned his quarters last. As long as he used his eyeglasses only for reading and left them off the rest of the time, he didn't much mind the state of his house trailer. If it got too bad, he could always sleep in the bed of his old Ford pickup, which even ran sporadically and had a trailer hitch. Still grieving over his lost "offerings" can, Tyrel labored to his feet. For all he knew, someone might have put a one hundred dollar bill in that can. Well, whatever it contained, it was lost and gone forever, he knew that.

Tyrel limped to the door and looked out. The lowering sun behind him cast long rods of gold through the reddening clouds and patches of pale blue. He saw that the ground was damp and realized that rain had come while he dozed. Stepping out into the sense-quickening smell of rain, Tyrel found himself pulled into the outside world, walking gingerly toward the road. He did not feel much like a prophet at the moment, at least not the way he thought a prophet, even a battered one, should feel—uplifted and sure. Downtrodden and confused was more how he felt. There sat his bicycle, its wheel and frame bent beyond repair with no raffle in sight. Unless he could get his truck running, he was afoot for the foreseeable future.

Marilyn Arnold

As he walked along the main road, Tyrel's mind turned to the mysterious note he had all but forgotten, the note that instructed him to visit the Carruth house and there ponder the message of the riddle. When he had solved it, he was to write his answer and leave it at the house. If he followed these instructions, it said, he would be rewarded with a treasure. Well, Tyrel allowed as how he had done a good deal of pondering of late, on the matter of Divine Capitalism and his calling to preach it. So he knew what pondering was, and he didn't see much point in doing any more of it unless there truly was some hard cash in it, or a chance at a new bicycle. "Absurd to the wise is deficient." He knew what absurd was when he saw it, and he knew it wasn't Tyrel K. Fernley. Tyrel, after all, was a chosen servant of the Lord, with a pipeline to divine wisdom and a gift for winning raffles. The farthest thing from absurd, or from deficient either, for that matter.

Tyrel had been so absorbed in thought that he was surprised to find himself in front of the Carruth house, which was a good half mile down the highway from the RV park where he lived. He stopped a long minute, kicked a loose rock or two, then started up the driveway. Tyrel wasn't exactly tuned in to local doings, he being extremely busy with the stock market and more recently with the responsibilities of his ministry; but he knew about the Carruth brothers all right. People still talked about how those two broke their parents' hearts and sent them sorrowing to the grave. And before the elder

Perfecting Amiable

Carruths were cold in the ground, the boys up and cut the house in half and then died underneath it. Tyrel faced the house and, raising the arm that wasn't splinted, made a solemn pronouncement: "A house divided against itself cannot stand." Tyrel knew a few biblical passages by heart, and that was one of them. He was pleased to find a use for it.

As he drew nearer the house, a familiar object caught his eye. There, perched on a large rock at the front corner of the house, was a Poppycock can. He knew without opening it that it was his and that it had been miraculously transported to where he was. When he opened it and found a ten-dollar bill inside, he took it as a sign. There was also a note, which he barely made out in the approaching dusk: "Render unto Caesar that which is Caesar's." Feeling a bit weak, Tyrel took the can to the rear of the house and slowly lowered himself, glassy-eyed, onto the back steps. He knew who said that about Caesar originally. The same person who taught the Gospel of Divine Capitalism in the parable of the talents—Jesus. Tyrel thought and thought, but he couldn't reconcile the two. To the best of his recollection, that same person also said things like "where your treasure is, there will your heart be also," and "consider the lilies of the field." None of those others sounded to him like Jesus was very interested in money or the things money could buy. Then why did Jesus throw in that parable about investments? Was he trying to trick people, or what?

Marilyn Arnold

Weary though he was, Tyrel did not sleep well that night. He tossed fitfully from his back to his right side. He could not lie on his left side bcause that arm ached; and sharp pain pierced through it at any quick movement. In the middle of the night another truth hit him, simultaneously with a stabbing pain in his left arm. People were laughing at him. Not everybody, maybe, but some. The smart ones were laughing because he had got the parable all wrong! Maybe Jesus wasn't talking about making money after all. Maybe he didn't care about money, or raffles either. Maybe Jesus was talking about what we do with ourselves! "The smart ones," Tyrel intoned out loud, "the smart ones are laughing." And then he knew the meaning of the riddle. Painfully he left his makeshift bed, turned on the weak overhead light, tore the membership page off his notebook, and on the back deciphered the riddle.

The next day he walked again to the Carruth house where he pressed his little treatise under a piece of loose siding near the front. Then he walked into town and applied for work at Sally's Saloon and Grill—graveyard shift. Sally was reluctant at first, given Tyrel's reputation and his broken arm, but then she relented. So Brionna Lee Wells wouldn't be there alone in the dark of night, she said. After that, Tyrel walked over to the water and electric works branch office and opened an account with a ten-dollar deposit. "No," he told the clerk, "you don't need t' connect the lines. You just need t' read the meters out t' the RV park."

Six

LaDessa Bernadine Payton was in a royal tizzy; but since tizzy was more or less her usual state, her husband Alvin didn't pay much attention to it. Luckily, he was an easygoing fellow, and the years had taught him to reduce his wife's emotional hailstorms to spring showers. It was his way of being supportive. LaDessa knew that, but she still found herself wishing that just once in a while he would get all worked up about something, so she'd have company. The two were opposites, in temperament and in nearly every other way. They claimed it made for a happy marriage. People said that if both of them had LaDessa's flamboyance and her gift for browbeating people into doing what she wanted, the roof would have blown off their modest stucco home thirty years ago. It was a great mystery to the town that the three Payton children turned out normal and well-adjusted. The neighbors credited Alvin, of course, who must have immunized the offspring against their mother's legendary hysteria.

The problem was that LaDessa Bernadine was theatrical, and not just a smidgen theatrical either, but in the most extravagant and irrepressible sense of the term. Now certainly, large and even not so large cities can absorb theatrical persons, and life pretty much goes on with little ado. Amiable, however, was not a city of any kind, and therefore, it was a place where just one theatrical person could stir up a good deal of ado over not very much. Shakespeare got it oh, so right. Then too, maybe a small town in Connecticut, or New Hampshire, or Maine, places more accustomed to artsy, "expressive" characters, would have taken LaDessa in stride. But an isolated western town surrounded by turkey farmers and cattle ranchers could not. No one could figure out how Amiable had spawned such a person as LaDessa— after all, she was a native daughter—and why Alvin Payton courted her and won her when everyone could see from the time she was six years old that she was theatrical. They just didn't know she was going to be as bad as she was.

Nonetheless, some had to admit that at first it was rather nice, in a way, to have someone like LaDessa on hand to volunteer for things that anybody else would have to be bent over

Perfecting Amiable

a barrel and arm-twisted into doing. But then it got to be a problem because once LaDessa was entrenched in the business of civic observances and entertainments, she expected to orchestrate virtually every important public event ever held, from the annual spring garden and fashion show to the Amiable Musical Theater production every fall in the high school auditorium. She also did the Christmas pageant at the Community Church and the Easter egg hunt, and she had hinted that she was prepared to take over the rodeo at a moment's notice. People were surprised when she didn't wrest Tyrel Fernley's revival meeting away from him one way or another. Then it was learned that when Tyrel was performing, LaDessa and Alvin had been out of town, visiting their son's family, and therefore had missed it entirely. Some said she took to her bed at the news.

To date, no mayor had mustered the courage to appoint anyone else to head up even one of these enterprises, and when LaDessa received a telephone call from the mayor's office the Thursday after Tyrel's fiasco, she knew what it was for. Over the years, the sitting mayors had observed these little formalities, and she rather enjoyed them herself. On this occasion, she had just successfully carried off the Fourth of July picnic, band concert, and fireworks extravaganza, and now the mayor was certainly about to persuade her, over her rehearsed modest protests, that she was the only one in town with the wit and skills to direct and star in this season's musical.

Marilyn Arnold

Of all the productions LaDessa organized and directed, the annual musical was her favorite. It was the high point of her year. So far, however, she had not received her formal invitation from the current mayor. When it came, it would, as always, give her unimpeachable authority to initiate tryouts and conduct rehearsals. Of course, there was never a tryout for female lead. She always sang that. Last year she was Marian the Librarian in *The Music Man*, and she had already decided to do *The Sound of Music* again this year since it was such a crowd favorite. She would play Maria, of course, and she'd make certain the high school music teacher won the part of Captain von Trapp.

LaDessa was careful to choose only those musicals that would showcase her talents. All agreed that her voice was as good as ever, though some said that was no advantage because it never was very good. As the years went by, however, things grew increasingly awkward with her playing the romantic lead, generally against a much younger man. Every year this became more problematic because every year LaDessa aged another twelve months. People were somewhat relieved to hear what she was planning to produce this year; at least the male lead would be out of his twenties.

No one could forget the disaster two years ago when LaDessa, then fifty if she was a day, played the young daughter whose marriage is celebrated in *Fiddler on the Roof*, while the person who played her mother was far

Perfecting Amiable

younger than she was. Unfortunately, the unsophisticated Amiable audience was unable to suspend its disbelief indefinitely, and several persons burst into uncontrollable laughter during the couple's tenderest love scene. Who could blame them? After all, there on the stage was young Jerry Lee Mumford talking sweet talk to a woman more than twice his age, doing his best to keep a straight face and more than likely wishing he was somewhere else—anywhere. In a den of lions. At the dentist. He discovered what every adult knows, that pain is relative.

Needless to say, although LaDessa probably thought she was prepared for the conversation that ensued when she arrived at Mayor Dorsen Ruckles' office Friday morning, she was not. She was dressed to the nines, as they say, and her perfume was so strong it made Dorsen lightheaded. Dorsen was a rather large man, thick and tall, but that didn't mean he was fearless. After all, he was only a part-time mayor. The rest of the time he sold automobile and life insurance from his house on Third Street.

"Mornin', Miz Payton," he crowed with manufactured bravado, putting out a broad hand to shake her lean one. "Mighty glad y' could come in."

"Why, Mayor Ruckles," LaDessa twittered, curtsying grandly and ignoring the hand, "I'm always at the beck and call of my mayor, whoever he happens to be." (In Amiable it was always a he.) "I've seen a lot of mayors in my day," she reminded him.

Dorsen retracted his hand and began rubbing both palms together. "Well, uh, Miz Payton, seems it's time t' start talkin' turkey about th' upcomin' fall musical." He went behind his desk. "Uh, siddown, wouldja?" He motioned toward a chair that faced the desk. It was a dark, wooden affair with worn arms and nearly threadbare seat pad.

LaDessa frowned momentarily as she contemplated the chair. It had not been replaced in more than twenty years. "Surely, Mayor," she said scornfully, "our taxes could provide another chair or two for the mayor's office. After all, we must put our best foot forward, mustn't we?"

Dorsen coughed nervously and sat behind his desk. He looked out the window. "Uh, glad you feel that way, Miz Payton. Them's my thoughts prexactly. We gotta put our best foot forward." He hesitated. "Uh, I've been thinkin' . . . uh, that is, some of us've been thinkin' that maybe you'd like it if somebody else done . . . uh, did, the show this fall." He paused again. "It's such a lotta work and all. An' you've done it fer so long . . . uh, we've imposed on you fer so long . . ."

LaDessa's face turned ashen. "Someone else do the musical!" she exclaimed at last. "Why, I've never heard of such a thing. I've always done the musical. Who on earth could do it?"

Perfecting Amiable

"Well, I don't rightly know at this point. We ain't picked anybody yet, but we thought maybe Fawnine Winkel . . . because she teaches speech and drama over t' the high school. Not necessarily t' perform, y' understand, but t' kinda put it together." Mayor Ruckles stood and walked to the window. "An' then there's that young woman's come t' town, that new kindergarten teacher. I've heard her sing over t' church, an' she's purty darned good." He waited, then turned back. "Whut's her name, now? Luetta is it? She could do a bang-up job as a leadin' lady."

"Luetta Rae Forbush," LaDessa said blackly.

"Yeah, that's it. Forbush. Anyhow, we ain't asked her yet neither." Dorsen cleared his throat. "Uh, wanted t' run it by you first."

After a long silence, LaDessa looked him squarely in the eye. "Well, you've run it, and the answer is no. When I'm ready to give up the musical theater, I'll tell you. Until then, you'll just have to endure me." Having said that, she arose with a flourish and flounced out of the office. "The idea!" she exclaimed as she passed the part-time secretary. "They can't do this to me. You tell him that. They can't do this to me."

LaDessa was still fuming when Alvin got home that evening. Alvin ran a little plumbing shop, but his avocation was peacekeeping. He practiced it with all the devotion of a novitiate entering a holy order. People wondered how he did it. Some even called him a saint, though others thought that was stretching it. Good old Alvin, as the town had dubbed him, was accustomed to being LaDessa's audience, both at home and abroad, but just now even he couldn't seem to calm her. Over the years he had learned that what sometimes turned the tide was a long walk to the edge of town and back, if he could talk her into it. As a rule, LaDessa wasn't much for exercise, unless you count flying off the handle. She always said she had a delicate constitution, and too much exercise gave her the hives. Of course, she could endure late night rehearsals and endless performances of all kinds with no ill effects whatsoever. What she couldn't endure was having her will crossed.

In any event, Alvin was able to persuade her to walk with him on the evening in question. He pleaded with her on the grounds that he needed to get out, to clear his head. It would be a great favor to him, he said. Since he put it that way, she responded; she couldn't refuse. She would be the martyr, put aside her own anguish for the sake of her dear husband. All in all, it was one of her better performances. Two or three neighbors were on their front porches when the Paytons came along, and LaDessa was pleased to inform them of the great wrong done her. Hollis Beacham was sweeping the walk in front of his hotel, and she treated him to the tragic tale of her visit to the mayor's office. The girls were just closing the Mercantile as LaDessa and Alvin walked by, and so

Perfecting Amiable

naturally they also became a captive audience. When Mrs. Ransom pulled up to ask if the Paytons needed a ride somewhere, LaDessa unburdened her soul further.

Yes indeed, it was a gratifying experience, that evening walk. LaDessa was brilliant. She played the ill-used heroine of her own drama with as much passion as she played Lady Macbeth. By the time she and Alvin reached home, she felt that the whole town had sided with her and against the mayor and his cronies, those conniving men on the city council who had plotted against her. She would produce the musical, she would star in it as always, and as always she would carry away the accolades. She was invincible. No one could touch her. In a gratuitous gesture, she allowed Alvin to hold her hand for the last quarter mile, and to kiss her goodnight at bedtime.

LaDessa figured that things would quiet down over the weekend, that the mayor would repent of his ill-conceived plan to replace her and would beg her forgiveness on bended knee. Thus, it was no surprise to her when a letter from the mayor's office, delivered by courier, arrived at her door Monday morning. She knew what it would say. He would apologize for behaving boorishly (though he wouldn't use that word) and beg her to organize and once again direct the fall musical. Smiling with self-satisfaction, LaDessa opened the official envelope. As she read, her face fell a good inch, and she reached to the dining table for support. Slumping into a chair, she read the letter again, thinking she had misunderstood. A second reading confirmed that she had not. This is what it said:

Dear Mrs. Payton:

As of our conversation of yesterday, to wit, relieving you of all duties pertaining to the Amiable fall musical, this letter is to confirm that you have hereby and hereinafter been relieved. Miss Fawnine Winkel has agreed to step into your very large shoes. We thank you for your envious past service and wish you happiness in your future endeavors, whatever they may be.

Yours truly,

Dorsen Ruckles, Mayor of Amiable, and

City Council of Amiable

P.S. Please ask Alvin to come to city hall ASAP. We have a leaky toilet.

At first, LaDessa was so stunned she could only lie on the couch with a cold compress on her head, but when she got her strength back she invested it in righteous indignation. She knew just where to begin her campaign for reinstatement—the Cuts 'n Curls. She'd find many a sympathetic ear in the beauty salon. Why, she could stir up enough sentiment in this town to get the mayor impeached. For that matter, she might even nominate Alvin, or herself, to replace him. Give the town a grammatical mayor for the first time in its anything but illustrious history. Then we'd see who would produce and star in the fall musical.

"What'd you say, honey?" Leola Baxter said as she simultaneously chewed a large wad of gum and rolled a strand of Edna Fay Boyack's reddish hair up to her scalp on a pink plastic roller. She was talking to LaDessa Payton who had just come in, muttering the pitiful song of the mad, rejected Ophelia. The Monday afternoon regulars were on hand at the Cuts 'n Curls when LaDessa arrived. The weekend had been rather slow for most of them, so they were delighted when LaDessa came waltzing in the front door. They knew they were in for a show.

LaDessa sized up her audience. "I'm going to impeach that worthless mayor of ours!" she cried, moving to center stage between the hair dryers and the styling chairs.

"Why, whatever for, LaDessa?" Edna Fay asked. "I thought you an' him got on famous."

"We did get on. That's in the past tense."

"What's a past tense, honey?" Leola asked.

Edna Fay was quick to show her learning. "It means somethin' that ain't no longer," she explained.

LaDessa struck a tragic pose. "His royal majesty has informed me that my professional services are no longer required."

"Huh? Whut services?" Elja Nexel was apparently still in the dark.

At that moment, Delsene Parmley walked in the back door from the parking area. LaDessa was glad to see her because of her reputation as a gossip with a gift for embellishment. Of late, however, it seemed as if no one could get a word out of Delsene unless it was something nice. Everyone was wondering what had happened to her, and more than a few speculated that somebody had threatened her with a lawsuit, although that had never stopped her before.

"Do come in, Delsene," said Carlynn Ingles. "LaDessa's about to start impeachment proceedings against our noble mayor." Carlynn was prone to show off her college education, even if it was only by correspondence courses advertised in a magazine she saw in a dentist's office in Sage.

Ignoring Carlynn, LaDessa returned to Elja's question. "I am no longer wanted as producer and star performer for the Amiable Musical Theater," she announced grandly.

The women were stunned. No one would have guessed. This was news. LaDessa painted a tale of a heartless Dorsen Ruckles, first berating her in person, then tearing her to shreds in a followup letter. She began to weep.

"I'm a worthless has been," she sobbed, "unfit even to live, much less to direct or sing." She paused for effect, glancing at the stricken faces around her. "I've been thrown to the wolves!" she cried, then collapsed in the center stylist's chair that was vacant at the moment. "My life is over!"

The women at the Cuts 'n Curls were all sympathy. They weren't particularly fond of the mayor, anyway, though their husbands all voted for him. They seemed glad for a specific reason to dislike him. Of course, up to this moment LaDessa hadn't exactly been on their love lists either. Some of them had even made fun of her singing voice in the past. But oh, how they could leap to the defense of a sister wronged by a male chauvinist. It was a beautiful thing to see.

"Why, who'll direct if you don't?" one cried.

"An' who'll sing the main lady's part?" asked another.

LaDessa threw her head back as though in utter disbelief herself. "Fawnine Winkel will direct!" she exclaimed. "That woman without an ounce of stage sense, much less experience with adults!"

"Well, it would make some sense," mumbled Lula Greene, the bank teller who was getting a trim. All eyes turned disapprovingly on Lula. "But only if LaDessa can't do it, of course," she added hastily.

"She'll sing, too? I didn't know Fawnine could sing," Elja said.

"She can't," LaDessa said haughtily. "Luetta Rae Forbush" will sing the female lead."

"Ohhh," they all murmured. "Well, doesn't that take the cake. She's a pretty little thing, ain't she?"

"Hmmph! If you like the type," LaDessa sniffed, then

stalked out, nearly colliding with Mrs. Ransom who was distributing flyers to local businesses about an upcoming clothing drive.

As she drove home, LaDessa didn't rate her mission to the beauty shop as an unqualified success, but she knew it would accomplish her purpose. Word would soon be all over town about the terrible injustice that had been done her. She also vowed not to tell Alvin about the leaky toilet in city hall.

The next morning when LaDessa went outside to water the geraniums in a planter beside her front steps, her daily ritual, whether the flowers needed water or not, she noticed a folded slip of paper under one corner of the planter box. Curious, she picked it up and unfolded it. The paper contained the same instructions delivered in earlier messages to various townspeople, though naturally LaDessa didn't know that. She was told to visit the Carruth house alone and ponder the maxim printed below. When she arrived at some insight as to how the saying applied to herself, she was to write what she discovered on a piece of paper and leave it at the Carruth house. A treasure awaited her if she solved the riddle. The problem was, the so-called maxim made no sense. It sounded like something familiar, but she couldn't make heads or tails of it. This is what it said, in capital letters:

A ROLLING THRONE GATHERS NO GLOSS.

Perfecting Amiable

To an audience of geraniums and possibly a lizard or two, LaDessa made it plain that she did not appreciate in the slightest someone's tampering with her psyche. She crumpled the paper in her left hand and stomped into the house.

The more LaDessa thought about it, the more upset she became. "Wild horses couldn't drag me to that sick excuse of a house," she informed the parakeet as she passed. "The nerve of somebody, trying to get inside my head. Who do they think they are?" Her first thought was that the note came from the mayor, but then she realized that it was written in standard English, a form of discourse with which the mayor was not personally acquainted. Nor was he likely ever to be, at least not in this life. And his part-time secretary was no better. A faithful disciple she was, in the Dorsen Ruckles Academy of Freestyle Expression and Grammar.

LaDessa's day was pretty much a loss after she found and read the message. True enough, she received a few phone calls, all from women who had performed with her or for her in the past. Oh, they were appropriately aghast, appalled, and dismayed. If she said the word, they would march on town hall, or burn the mayor in effigy. Women, generally, are very good at verbally commiserating with other women, even if in their secret hearts they feel some guilty pleasure at a rival's being brought down. In fact, the inner satisfaction they feel can give a certain verve to their outward sympathy. They can now afford to be generous.

Alvin was out on a job all morning, so she was unable to ruin his day any further. Moreover, he was going fishing that afternoon with Owen Prattly, their minister, and wouldn't be home until dark. LaDessa knew Alvin deserved some time off. He was hard-working and had few diversions other than her performances and productions. She, on the other hand, was always off somewhere, in committee meetings, at rehearsals—you name it. And Alvin never complained. Therefore, she could not complain, or even whine more than a little. What this meant, however, was that LaDessa would be alone part of the evening as well as all afternoon. Time. With time on her hands now, she was beginning to feel desperate. Finally, shortly after six, she snatched up her car keys and dashed out the door. In a flash she was back in the house, then out again, clutching the mysterious note in her hand.

This was the first time LaDessa had seen the Carruth house up close since the fatal day the two brothers brought half of it down on their own heads. Naturally, LaDessa had a front row view of that production. That she could have scripted it better than the Carruth boys did goes without saying. She could have spiced up the whole thing, made it something that would have given people nightmares for years. Now here she was, on that same ground, with orders not to spice

Perfecting Amiable

but to ponder. Not just any old thing, either, but some nonsensical riddle that some deranged person concocted for her particular torment. She asked herself how a normal, sane person with an above average IQ, and considerable musical and organizational gifts, could sit next to half a house and ponder one tiny inane sentence for more than ten seconds running. How did she let this thing get to her, this ridiculous anonymous message? Feeling more foolish by the minute, LaDessa started the engine on her gray Saturn, backed onto the long brown grass, lurched into drive, and sped for the highway. She dearly hoped that no one saw her.

LaDessa was sitting on the porch swing when Alvin pulled his white Chevy pickup into the driveway. She called to him as he opened the truck door, and he came over, fishing pole and tackle box in hand.

"Catch anything?" she asked.

"Nothing big enough to keep."

"Good, then you won't have to clean fish tonight."

"And you won't have to cook fish tomorrow."

Alvin set his pole and tackle on the porch floor and sat heavily next to his wife. Reaching out to pat her knee, he squinted at her face in the dim light filtering through the window. "Are you all right?" he asked quietly.

She stared off into space. "No, I'm not all right," she said. "Am I supposed to be?" LaDessa had decided she would not tell Alvin about the mysterious note, and not because it had instructed her to keep mum, either. In her mind, the note made her look bad. She had been singled out as some kind of "case" that needed changing. She saw it as an attempt to get her to acknowledge some flaw, though she wasn't sure what. One thing was certain: she didn't like it a bit. Not a bit.

Alvin leaned back and rested his head on the swing cushion. "You know, you could just let it all go," he said. "You've given so much over the years. Maybe it's time to slow down and let life catch up with you. You know, bow out gracefully."

"Hmmph! Sounds like you're on their side!"

Alvin chuckled softly. "No, I'm on your side. I've always been on your side." He paused. "I just want you to be happy. There's more to happiness than having things your way, than being in charge. You don't have to be on stage to shine."

"You've never said things like this before. What's got into you? Don't I suit you any more?"

He stood, made a deep bow before her, and extended his hand. "Suit me? Why, madam, have I ever complained? And now, may I have this dance?"

LaDessa looked at her husband quizzically, hesitantly, then stood and curtsied. "Why, yes, noble sire," she responded in her most elegant southern accent, "you may certainly have this dance." Then she smiled and added,

Perfecting Amiable

"Even if you do smell like fish and river mud."

The next morning, after Alvin had gone off to work, LaDessa grabbed a notebook and ball point pen and headed for the divided house. Last night, after Alvin went to bed, she had sat a good while on the porch, thinking. Well, she told herself, if that house has something to say to me, it better say it quick and in plain English. I really must be a basket case if I'm taking any of this foolishness seriously. She savored the fact that she had purposely not informed Alvin of the leaky toilet at city hall. That proved she had not totally lost her will or her mind.

Parked once more beside the abandoned monument to pride and stubbornness, LaDessa opened the car door, walked to the rear of the house, and sat on the back steps. Trained to the theater and its magic, her mind began producing "what might have been," as she saw in her imagination the house, newly painted and whole, with climbing roses on trellises and freshly mowed grass. She saw outbuildings in good repair, and a modern tractor rolling in from the field. Two brothers greeted each other warmly and shared lunch on a log under the shade of the big cottonwood tree. And then a sound broke into the picture, sweet, warbling, high-pitched. The sound was real—not imagined. Two rosy-headed house finches atop the crumbling shed were broadcasting their immeasurable joy to the heavens.

Marilyn Arnold

LaDessa had forgotten that very common little birds could sing uncommonly, pouring out their hearts whether they had an audience or not. She looked around her. There by the steps, behind the spent hollyhocks, were wild roses, fragrant, delicate; and farther out sunflowers, common as grass, all blooming untended, unseen, unappreciated. How long had it been since she stopped to listen to a bird or to admire a flower that many regarded as a weed? Alvin had talked last night about letting go of things tied up with ego—yes, though he didn't say the word, it's what he meant—ego, self. And with that letting go might come the opening of the self to other things, other possibilities, other experiences. What might be a dull blur in the constant strife for power and attention could actually take on a sheen in repose. "A rolling throne gathers no gloss." As LaDessa repeated the riddle she was instructed to solve, she remembered a line from Milton, who had lost his eyesight but gained something else: "They also serve who only stand and wait."

Scarcely conscious of time passing, LaDessa became aware that the sun was burning down on her from overhead. Instinctively, she moved out of the sun to the shade of the big cottonwood, to the spot where she had imagined a reconciled Thoral and Thurlin Carruth sharing a peaceful lunch in their break from the day's labor. Taking out the notebook and pen she had brought, LaDessa wrote something on the

Perfecting Amiable

top sheet, then folded it and tucked it deep in the heavy bark of the cottonwood. Then she drove home to telephone Alvin about a plumbing problem in city hall.

Seven

It was widely assumed around Amiable that after Lavoid W. Perkins' parents died and left him alone with all those turkeys, he had gone daffy, or as Elja Nexel put it, daffy-down-dilly. Lavoid, a lean, wiry man with something of a paunch and thinning brown hair, knew what people thought, and they could go hang for all he cared. He had always been more at home with turkeys than people anyway. His father, Merton L. Perkins, introduced him to turkey farming when he was three years old, and it was all he had ever known. The youngest of four children, Lavoid came along as a midlife surprise to his fifty-two-year-old parents. None of his older siblings had taken to turkeys, and

Perfecting Amiable

that left him to fulfill his father's dream.

Lavoid had almost no recollection of his three sisters and one brother because they had left the farm one by one when he was just a toddler—as soon as they scraped up enough money for bus tickets. Oh, they came to Amiable once in a while, if their consciences got to working on them; and they called on the phone to say hello to their mother. But they generally avoided their father because they weren't comfortable with guilt. And after their parents were gone, they avoided Lavoid for the same reason. Then, too, they were old enough to be his parents. They never really knew him. His name described the relationship, if you leave off the "L." Some said his name also described his life, "la" meaning "the" in Spanish. No matter that "la" was the feminine form, his name still said "the void."

Well, it was really okay with him that the others left for good. That way he didn't have to divide the property with them when his mother and father passed on. He inherited the farm and all the turkeys, which suited the others just fine, and went a long way toward assuaging their guilt. He thought it too bad that the Carruth brothers didn't have it easy the way he did, with no disputes over who gets what. He didn't know what anybody would do with half a house.

Everybody said Lavoid was married to those birds of his and would never take a wife—but he fooled them. He did take a wife, eventually, and maybe he fooled her, too. Maybe she thought she was getting a bargain. Of course, Lavoid never liked to rush into things. He waited until he was forty-five to go courting, and then he settled on a woman who was forty-nine and desperate and had never heard of him. He had to go to the next county to find one who qualified. He wanted a wife without the built-in biases against him and his turkeys that ran in the drinking water around Amiable. Everybody wondered how a wife would feel, playing second fiddle to a bunch of brainless turkeys.

Lavoid's courtship is a story in itself. He didn't follow customary procedures. Although he attended Amiable public schools, he never socialized much. Oh, he went to a football game or two, and even a dance once with a girl who asked him, but all he thought about through those trying experiences was getting home to the turkeys. He hated it when people used the word "turkey" in a demeaning way because in his mind to be called a turkey was a high compliment. Regardless of local speculation, it wasn't lonesomeness or testosterone that ultimately drove Lavoid to take a bride; it was a craving for domestic help. He considered hiring a girl or a woman to keep house for him, but then he thought to himself, why pay someone to do what a wife would do for free? Of course, he would have to feed her, but if he got a thin wife she wouldn't eat all that much.

Perfecting Amiable

It wasn't as though he'd have to fatten her for market, either.

Lavoid chewed the matter over for several weeks, weighing the pros and cons. Then he made up his mind. The pros outweighed the cons. The big question was how to go about it. He had never courted before and had no one to consult but the turkeys. They, he could see, had a great advantage because of their natural gregariousness. If he could have trained one to keep house, he'd have been happy to die a bachelor. More than happy. He didn't need any of that sweet talk. Contented turkey gobbling was music to his ears, though not to everyone's. Even so, people could more or less ignore the low-pitched, every day gabble of Lavoid's birds. If a coyote happened by on a summer night, however, the gobblers set up a clatter people couldn't ignore, especially those who lived south of town and slept with their windows open or were blessed with sleeping porches.

Once his mind was made up, Lavoid didn't waste any time. He was already in line the next morning when stacks of the *Sage Star Review* were delivered to the hotel, the Merc, the Gas and Go, and the eating establishments. His eyes were a little bleary because he had spent half the night composing and recomposing a piece for the "Personals" section of the classified ads. Even as he waited for the delivery van from Sage, Lavoid reworked his little composition. His plan was to read all the personal ads in the current edition, and with that research under his belt, make a final draft and drive the eighty miles to Sage where he would hand deliver his composition. He would not trust it to the mails. Lavoid rented a post office box before delivering his ad to the newspaper. He didn't want anybody in Amiable connecting him with the ad. He would drive to Sage once a week to clear the box. This is the ad as it appeared in the *Star Review*:

Dedicated middle-afed farmer seeks thin wife under 50 who liks turkeys and is willing to cook and lean house. Require housekeeping experience but not wife experince. Interested parties may respond to P.O. Box 319, Sage, Utah.

Lavoid got more than he bargained for. It turned out that there were more desperate women on the loose in Sage and thereabouts than he would have imagined. He apparently also raised the hackles of a few neo-feminists who weren't shy about telling him what for. Below is a representative sampling of his correspondence:

Dear farmer:
How thin is thin? I am 50 and single, but I've never likked turkeys, so I don't noe about that. What does it entale? My frends say I'm nice looking and a good cook.

Perfecting Amiable

Dear Sir:

I hope all the spelling errors in your ad are the news-paper's fault and not yours. I could never marry a man with such a deplorable command of the English language. If the copy you submitted was flawless, you may call me to discuss possible marriage terms.

Dear Mister:

How many turkeys are we talking about? Would they be allowed in the house? I don't mind a turkey out-side, but I won't stand for turkey dung in my house. My first husband, rest his soul, had a goat. Are turkeys as bad as goats?

Dear whoever you are:

I'm 52 and not especially thin, but I'm jolly. At least that's what people say. If you want a jolly wife, I'm it. A joy to be around. What does cooking matter if your wife is a joy to be around?

Dear Sir:

I must say you've got your nerve, advertising for a virtual household slave! No woman in her right mind would answer your ad. The days of woman's servi-tude are over, or hadn't you heard?

Marilyn Arnold

Dear lover-boy:
I'm it, reddy to be your little sweaty-pie. Forget those noisy ol' turkeys and cuddle up with me. So what if I'm a little chunky? After too minutes, you won't even notiss. I promiss.

It was a discouraged Lavoid Perkins who shuffled out of the Sage Post Office and into a nearby diner. Finding a suitable wife was going to be harder than he thought. Fortunately, he had no delusions about finding true love. He sat in the far booth, head in hands, for a good many minutes. At last, a waitress in blue jeans and lavender tunic brought a menu, which he ignored. She returned several minutes later, but the menu was still unopened.

"C'n I getcha somethin'?" she asked, shifting her gum to the other side of her mouth.

Lavoid judged her to be in her early twenties. Too young, he thought, and too sloppy. He waved her off.

She left, but returned with ice water. "Coffee?" she asked. He shook his head.

"Look, mister, if y' gonna eat y' c'n stay. If not, I got other things t' do."

He looked up, something of a dazed expression on his face. "You married?" he asked.

She was taken aback. "Who me? Whut's it t' you?"

Lavoid fixed his eyes on the table top, on his folded hands.

134

Perfecting Amiable

"I'm lookin' for a wife," he said, "a thinnish middle-aged wife who c'n cook." He paused. "And who don't mind turkeys."

"This ain't no marriage bureau. Do I look like some fancy matchmaker?"

Lavoid seemed confused. "No, no . . . I didn't mean . . . I only meant . . ."

The waitress' expression softened, and she sat down across from him. "Lookee here, mister, maybe I c'n help after all. I got this aunt, see, an' she ain't never married, but she wishes she had. She ain't real fussy, neither, an' she cooks pretty good. She's goin' to this here picnic tonight, with the Mormons. It's fer all them single folks what's on the prowl," the waitress added with a grin.

Lavoid shook his head. "No, no, we've got a few a' them in Amiable, too. I'm scairt a' them. Besides, them women over there tease me about smellin' like turkeys."

"I don't see what it could hurt if you wont. Nobody knows you. They don't know it's turkeys y' smell like. Tell 'em it's some cool new cologne."

And that's how Lavoid Perkins found a wife. Her name was Mirtis Fannin, and she was a native of Sage. He screwed up his courage and went to the picnic. When he saw her there, wearing a name tag and serving up Dutch oven potatoes, he thought maybe she could fill the bill. He lay in wait for her, and when she left the potatoes he went right up to her and started a conversation—something he had never done before in his life. Need and frustration had emboldened him.

"S'cuse me," he said, "you married?"

She looked at him. "Would I be here if I was?"

"D' you wanna be married?"

"Would I be here if I didn't?"

Lavoid paused. He wasn't sure he wanted to marry a woman who answered questions with questions. "D' you like turkeys?"

"Is that what I can smell?"

"Yeah. I grow 'em."

"I guess there's worse things."

Those were the magic words. Within weeks Lavoid had a full-time cook and housekeeper, which allowed him to devote full time to his turkeys. Some people said he slept with the turkeys before he was married, and maybe after, too, that it was part of the pre-nuptial agreement. But that was regarded by more sensible folks as an exaggeration. Leola Baxter down at the Cuts 'n Curls allowed as how such an arrangement was in the wife's best interest anyhow, given the powerful turkey smell that permeated the skin and defied even the best after shave lotion and masculine cologne. Not that Lavoid ever used those products. Leola maintained that his sense of smell had been permanently compromised ("wrecked" is the word she used) and she hoped to high

Perfecting Amiable

heaven his wife's had, too, before she moved to a turkey farm in Amiable.

People thought that maybe marriage would change Lavoid, soften him toward humankind and harden him a little toward turkeys. Some even claimed to have seen tears in his eyes when he shipped a truckload of his beloved birds to market. His only consolation lay in pulling a batch of new little ones from the incubators. Lavoid comforted himself with the fiction that the feeder turkeys knew when it was their time to go, and assented to it. And he believed firmly in a turkey heaven near the human one where he and the slaughtered (he hated that word) turkeys would one day be reunited. The way to a peaceful conscience, he found, was in loving the turkeys in the aggregate rather than as individuals. In any event, the hatching brood stayed around considerably longer, which made bonding the feeder birds to their fates less painful

People looked for change in Lavoid, yes, but they saw little evidence of it. Under the auspices of a friendly social call, a delegation of women from the Ladies League undertook a fact-finding mission to the Perkins farm to assess the new Mrs. Perkins. They didn't get past the front door. Mirtis Fannin Perkins said she had to take lunch out to her husband at that very minute and had no time for chit chat. On returning to town, the group stopped to make their report at the Cuts 'n Curls, where most of the local news originated or

137

got revisited and improved. Their comrades-in-helmets awaited them like sponges in dry flower pots.

"Well, she ain't much of a looker," Mattie Crumpla trumpeted as she burst through the front door. "Plain as the nose on yer face."

"Serves him right—him and his turkeys!" exclaimed Ruanna Molden, who was being permed. "He ain't changed a bit. Just got himself a slave."

"Oh, Lavoid's not so bad," Delsene Parmley volunteered from under the nearest dryer. "He works hard."

"Hmmph!" exclaimed Roxa Jane Biddell. "He won't love her half as much as he loves them birds. You should of went with us, t' see for yourself." Roxa Jane cast a critical eye on Delsene. "What's got into you, anyhow, Delsene Parmley? You plannin' to apply for sainthood? Where's all them juicy stories you used t' tell us?"

Delsene only smiled.

"Oh, don't pay her any mind, Roxa Jane," Leola Baxter said as she worked on Ruanna's perm. "Mebbe she's gone and got religion."

A few days after the visit of the Ladies League to the Perkins place, dreadful things began happening there, worse even than the ladies' visit. A swift and fatal disease began attacking Lavoid's turkeys. The first morning he found twenty dead, and by the next day another forty were gone.

Perfecting Amiable

They were dying faster than he could bury them. When the veterinarian arrived from Sage, he could only shake his head. He took blood samples and sent them off to a lab, but by the time the report came back, half the flock was gone. He tried putting medication in their water, but to no avail. Lavoid was beside himself. By week's end, every turkey on the place had died. He had no choice but to borrow a bulldozer from Elmo at the gravel pit, scoop out a great hole, and push the birds into it.

That done, Lavoid went into a deep depression. He locked himself in the granary and wouldn't come out. His wife Mirtis tried to reason with him through the door, but he wouldn't open it. He just told her to go away and leave him alone. She left food trays by the door, but the dogs usually got to them before Lavoid did. He was inconsolable. This went on for nearly two weeks. Then one Monday afternoon he emerged, gaunt and haggard, looking, in the local parlance, like death warmed over. Mirtis didn't seem to recognize him at first, which is explainable because she hadn't actually known him all that long. And even before the turkeys up and died, she hadn't really seen enough of him to memorize his features. When he got closer, though, she recognized the smell, enhanced now by two bathless weeks in the same clothes. He lumbered through the kitchen door, stomped over to the table, and dropped into a chair.

"Where's dinner!?" he demanded.

Marilyn Arnold

Mirtis left the sink from which she had watched his approach through the window. With hands on hips she stood over him, at least as close as she could get without swooning. For a good sixty seconds, she silently contemplated the living remains of the man she had married. "It's two p.m.," she said. "Dinner's at six."

"I want it now."

"My mother always said, "It isn't what you want that makes you fat, it's what you get," Mirtis replied. Then she softened. "I'm terribly sorry about those turkeys," she said. "Can you get some more?"

"Not while you're here. Them turkeys was fine 'til you come," he muttered. "They died a' broken hearts."

Mirtis stepped back even further. "Why, I never heard of such a thing. Turkeys are too dumb to know who's here and who's not. All they care about is getting fed and watered." She took a deep breath. "Like you," she sobbed and ran out of the room.

He banged around in the kitchen, eating everything in sight, then stomped out.

The next day when Lavoid marched up to the house at six, for supper, Mirtis was gone, as were her clothes and personal items. At his insistence, she had sold her car when she moved to Amiable—to save him money; so he supposed her sister came for her from Sage. The house felt oddly empty, which surprised him. After all, she hadn't been there all that long and

140

Perfecting Amiable

he hadn't spent all that much time with her. Still, she did make good dumplings, for a receptionist in a real estate office.

When a teetotaling, unimaginative man like Lavoid finds himself cruelly bereft of both turkeys and wife, his options are limited. The worst thing he could think of to do on this occasion was head for Sally's Saloon and Grill and drown his sorrows in beer, O'Doole's non-alcoholic variety. Sally had nursed him through a crisis or two in the past—one such crisis when a prankster turned half a dozen foxes loose among his turkeys, and another when somebody asked him, in all seriousness, why he didn't marry Delsene Parmley or Coral Watters.

After three or four O'Doole's, Lavoid was known to become talkative. It wasn't often that he came to the Saloon and Grill, even for a sandwich, so everyone knew that when he did come it was an event worth noting. Moreover, rarely did he drink any beverage with a tainted image. In his view, any liquid served at a bar had a tainted image, thereby making him feel dissolute and fallen when he imbibed. Dissolute and fallen is precisely how he wanted to feel on this occasion. As he downed the O'Doole's, he fancied himself getting drunk and so he began behaving as though he were drunk. Sally was there, dispensing sympathy as always, and charging Lavoid merely double the usual price for the virgin beer.

"M' turkeys'r gone," he blubbered. "Deader'n door-nails." He slammed his mug on the counter. "M' wife's gone, too. Deader'n a doornail."

"Hold on there, pardner," said Wilbert Wichen from the next stool. "You jus' got married, dintcha? Your wife dead a'ready?"

"Deader'n a doornail." Obviously, Lavoid liked the sound of the phrase. He repeated it several times.

Wilbert, who was only two sheets to the wind at this point, looked questioningly at Sally, who was tough as nails but looked for all the world like anybody's grandma. She was her own barkeeper and occasional short order cook. "Don't pay him no mind," she said. "His wife left him an' beat it back to Sage. Leastways that's where he thinks she's gone to."

Unnoticed by Lavoid, Mrs. Ransom had come in and taken a seat two stools down from him. She was reading the sandwich menu while Wilbert was commiserating with Lavoid. "I miss the turkeys th' mos'," Lavoid said. "We wuz blood brothers. Never shoulda married. Shoulda stuck with turkeys an' on'y turkeys. Too late now. They died 'cause she came. Thought I loved her more than them. Broke their little hearts."

"Fergit them turkeys," Wilbert advised, taking another swallow of brew. "I heard it was a virus, or mebbe pneumonia, that got 'em. Go bring that there woman back."

Perfecting Amiable

The next morning Lavoid awoke with a splitting headache. He may have been the only person in captivity who could charge a hangover to drinking non-alcoholic beer. Maybe it was the silence and not the O'Doole's that got to him. The turkeys had been stilled, and the only sound in the house was the ticking of his mother's parlor clock. It had never seemed so loud. He felt as though he were padding about in an echo chamber, or in the hollow of his own head. Staggering outside, Lavoid noticed that a folded piece of paper fluttered to the step landing when the screen door opened. Thinking it to be an advertising circular of some sort, or a notice of a change in watering turns, Lavoid picked it up and crammed it in his pocket, took a deep breath, and walked gingerly in his stocking feet to the water pump in the yard. Sometimes he doused his head there in the early morning to wake himself up, a habit he had picked up from watching John Wayne movies. Now that he thought about it, however, he couldn't recall whether John Wayne doused his head under a pump faucet, or with a bucket of well water. Perplexed, he shuffled back to the house undoused.

It wasn't until he sat down to eat a bowl of Wheaties and heard the crunch in his pocket that Lavoid remembered the piece of paper. Generally, he read the back of the cereal box while he ate breakfast; at least that's what he did before he married Mirtis and got cooked breakfasts to start his day.

Marilyn Arnold

Now it was back to cold cereal. On this occasion, he set the Wheaties box aside and extracted the paper from his pocket. It carried a strange message, the same message others had received, instructing him to go privately to the Carruth house and ponder a phrase printed in large capital letters. The note called it a maxim. When he had uncovered the meaning of the maxim, for him personally, he was to write it down and leave it at the Carruth house. If he did this, he would discover a treasure.

Lavoid didn't know if the note was intended to be a joke or a threat. One thing was certain, the maxim made no sense at all. This is what it said:

HOME IS WHERE THE SMART IS.

Lavoid was greatly perplexed. The saying had a familiar ring, and it didn't sound like something a prankster would trouble himself to think up. As for the promised treasure, Lavoid wasn't exactly a treasure hunter; but with all his turkeys wiped out, he could use a little treasure. He felt kind of foolish about following the instructions detailed in the note, but he asked himself what it could hurt and who would know anyway. Thus it was that within half an hour of finishing his Wheaties, Lavoid Perkins was parking his blue Dodge pickup alongside the Carruth house and cursing himself for being so gullible. Before the turkeys died he'd have

Perfecting Amiable

brushed the note off as a poor joke. But now, well, now he felt a little vulnerable, less sure of himself. Besides, he had a headache.

It was only the third time Lavoid had been on the Carruth property since Thoral and Thurlin Carruth cut the house in half and killed themselves. He remembered going there several years ago looking for a roll of baling twine he had lent Thoral. Another time, he went to scrounge around for salvageable wood. Week in and week out, he never thought of either brother any more—until right then. Right then, the full impact of what they had done hit him. "Those idiots!" he exclaimed aloud. "This silly ol' house was more important to 'em than each other. They tended that there grudge 'til it kilt 'em." He paused. "Oh, how them two loved that grudge," he muttered, opening the truck door and tramping through the long brown grass and weeds to the front of the house. "No wonder neither of 'em ever married." He paused. "No woman could compete with that grudge," he said in something close to a whisper.

Lavoid circled the house, wondering how some of the old irises had survived, choked as they were by weeds and grass, and starved for water. The saying on the paper kept surfacing in his mind: "Home is where the smart is." He shook his head. "The smart what?" he asked out loud. "Not the Carruth brothers, that's for sure." Lavoid slapped his hand against the back wall. "Those boys didn't have a home. What they had by that day was only a house. There's a difference." Still puzzled, Lavoid climbed into his truck and drove back to his farm—now a desolate graveyard. He wandered along the fence line, contemplating the empty coops and the silent ground once busy with noisy, scrabbling turkeys. Another thought came to him. The word "smart," it's got another meaning, too, don't it? A wound smarts.

Like a lost child, he stumbled into his house and walked slowly from room to room, touching the things Mirtis had added or changed, and staring a long time at his own image in the dresser mirror. It struck him as odd, almost frightening, that he found himself also missing Mirtis. The house had taken on a kind of glow after she moved in and brought it to life with flowers and new pictures and cushions and covers. Now the light seemed to have gone out of it, and out of him. He preferred to attribute his gloom wholly to the loss of his turkeys, but he couldn't quite convince himself that it was so. He hurt.

Lavoid sat a long hour on the ancient sofa, staring at the floor. Finally, he grabbed a notebook and pencil and bolted out the door. His tires spit a barrage of gravel as he spun out of his driveway and made for the Carruth house. There, after scribbling frantically for several minutes, he stuffed his composition behind the back steps and sped off for Sage.

Eight

Rilla Rowberry Ingersoll and her husband Herbert were
the nearest thing to royalty that Amiable could claim. They
were the town's undisputed upper crust, and Rilla never let
anyone forget it. She wore her husband's bank like a badge,
an entitlement to privilege. The fact that more than half the
people in town had mortgages and car loans and other debts
with Citizens Bank, and that it was the only bank around,
gave Rilla an enviable advantage over the other women. She
regarded herself as their superior, and even convinced some
of the more humble that she actually was.

Rilla was the only woman in town who could boast of a
son at Harvard and a daughter who was an attorney in

Marilyn Arnold

Chicago. She was not, however, the only woman who could boast of a son currently housed in the state penitentiary. But at least Rilla's son was incarcerated for sophisticated crimes like embezzlement and tax evasion, which was more than she could say for the other occasional jailbirds from Amiable, past and present. Most of them were guilty of more lowbrow crimes like drug possession and auto theft. In fact, the most common crimes around Amiable were poaching and jaywalking, which carried fines but didn't mean jail time.

Rather than subject herself weekly to what she regarded as the inferior skills of the hair stylists and the manicurists at the Cuts 'n Curls, when circumstances permitted, Rilla traveled the eighty miles to Sage for her shampoo-set and nail job. Besides, she found mingling with the women who frequented the local beauty shop rather distasteful. She had little interest in their conversations, and little tolerance for what she called "Amiable English." Moreover, she assumed that the women who frequented the Cuts 'n Curls sometimes talked of her in an admiring way, and she did not wish to "cramp their style" by her presence, as she told Herbert. She also made virtually all her purchases of nonperishable goods in Sage, or Las Vegas, or Salt Lake City rather than from local merchants. People said she operated under the mistaken notion that her husband's bank would benefit if he foreclosed on an unprofitable business.

Perfecting Amiable

Herbert Ingersoll was a local boy who had showed unusual promise. He went off to the nation's capital to get an education, and he returned with Rilla Rowberry, a tall slender woman whose features were rather severe even then. Herbert, a quiet man whose dark hair and moustache were now streaked with gray, seemed to regard her as an early symbol of his success, a prize to display. By the time he was forty, he owned the bank where he had begun as second vice president. Amiable was a far cry from Washington, D.C., and Rilla never let Herbert forget the sacrifice she had made in coming west with him. That fact gave her the leverage she needed to make him miserable for the rest of his life. But he fooled her. He was happy. People credited her for his success and wealth, on the grounds that he spent all his waking hours at work in order to avoid her company. The Ingersolls seemed to have an agreement: he would enjoy undisputed sovereignty in the bank, and she would enjoy undisputed sovereignty in the home. They might not have been lovebirds, but they respected each other's gifts and domains.

Today Rilla was still tall and slender, and impeccably groomed. She carried her age well, and people were even more afraid of her now than when she arrived in Amiable some thirty years earlier. At first, Herbert encouraged her to get acquainted with people, become part of the community. Then he simply stepped aside and let her go her own way.

Oh, she joined a small bridge group of closet Democrats, and even became friendly with one or two of them. The most intelligent of the group, and the one she liked best, turned out to be a Mormon; but poor Rilla didn't learn that disturbing fact until it was too late to reverse herself gracefully. If she had known earlier, she could have managed it. Certainly, life would be simpler for people like Rilla if Mormons wore the horns once ascribed to them. A woman of class could identify them and avoid them from the start.

Herbert, like most of the town, was a Republican. The locals always wondered what possessed him to marry Rilla and bring her to Amiable in the first place. Just as perplexing was what possessed her to come, much less to stay all these years. Knowing the two of them, folks really couldn't attribute either's decision to passion, nor to temporary insanity either. The Ingersolls were not the kind of people who lost their heads. Furthermore, they never spoke ill of each other, and their domestic help were said to be fiercely loyal to both of them.

What Rilla did with her time was something of a mystery to her neighbors. Clearly, it was not spent on domestic chores. A person of her breeding would never stoop to such. As a hedge against any sort of exposure of the Ingersolls' private lives, she hired domestic help from elsewhere, set them up in a nearby apartment, and conversed with them in Spanish, their native tongue. Another mystery was her children, who

Perfecting Amiable

were obviously reared under her influence and not their father's. There were a few skeptics who doubted their alleged accomplishments, arguing that Rilla had probably conferred advanced degrees on the older ones herself—by personal proclamation. After all, who had seen proof? All they had was her word for it.

Naturally, the skeptics never questioned the authenticity of reports about the Ingersoll son said to be serving time. After all, that was a story they wanted to believe. In fact, they enjoyed the story so much they kept adorning it with fantasies of their own. As a matter of fact, the townspeople never had much to do with the Ingersoll children because those children did not attend public schools after the sixth grade. Before they reached the age where they were allowed opinions of their own, they were shipped off to private eastern boarding schools where they learned just how superior they were in comparison with the run-of-the-mill residents of Amiable.

It was midsummer now, and Rilla and Herbert Ingersoll were planning their annual vacation abroad. That is, Rilla was planning their annual vacation abroad. Only she didn't use the word "vacation." She and Herbert, like their British counterparts, were going "on holiday." On this particular occasion, she had been to Sage consulting with her travel agent—she was not one to trust the internet on such matters, or on any other matters—and she was returning to Amiable with a front seat full of slick, full color brochures. Dusk was approaching when she guided her Cadillac Escalade down Main Street and turned sharply onto Oak Drive. As she swung around the corner, an open container of coke and ice that she had been nursing most of the way home flew out of the cup holder onto the brochures. Instinctively lurching and grabbing for the container, Rilla felt a hard thump in the vicinity of her right front wheel.

"Drat!"she exclaimed, straightening the steering wheel, "I've hit a big dog or a coyote! Why do people in this town let their dogs run loose? It's a wonder they aren't all dead!"

For half a moment, Rilla was tempted to go back and check, but she dismissed the idea. "All I can say is that my bumper or fender better not be damaged. It's good I was in this vehicle and not the sedan." Still, she was a little shaken. No one likes to hit an animal, especially in a new car, and her cars were always new. Herbert managed to get home for supper, which pleased her because she wanted to corner him after the meal and talk travel plans. In the flurry of brochures and flight schedules, the "thumping" incident was all but forgotten. Rilla went to bed with a clear conscience.

The next morning, she stopped at Herbert's bank to withdraw some cash from her checking account. Since the ATM machine was outside, she preferred to conduct her

Perfecting Amiable

business inside, with live tellers and in the presence of townspeople. In her view, it was a good reminder to bank clerks and townspeople in general that she was a person of some importance and position in Amiable. She was not to be taken lightly. Besides, she had a new hairdo and a shoulder bag full of travel brochures to exotic places, and both needed some public exposure if she was to reap full benefit from her trip to Sage. Quite frankly, Rilla enjoyed being envied. Certain things were meant for the public eye; others were not.

She even enjoyed having to wait in line for a teller because it gave her more personal display time, and on her terms. Of course, she needn't have gone to the bank at all. Herbert could have brought whatever cash she needed. He never questioned her expenditures or her management of domestic affairs. As Rilla stood at the counter preparing a withdrawal slip, Mrs. Ransom came into the bank and joined her. They knew each other, although not well, from one or two bridge gatherings in which Mrs. Ransom had substituted for one of the regulars. Mrs. Ransom, who lived alone but seemed to know everyone in town and played no favorites, greeted Rilla warmly. Rilla merely nodded.

As she endorsed several checks and filled out a deposit slip, Mrs. Ransom casually introduced a subject that was the current talk of Amiable. "Terrible thing, wasn't it, that hit-and-run last evening?"

Rilla didn't even look up. She found small talk with the locals tedious. "Oh, there was a hit-and-run? I hadn't heard." She yawned prettily.

"Why, yes, the little Murdock boy. He was struck by a vehicle just off Main Street. He must have run into the street without looking, or the driver was careless."

Rilla turned white and dropped the pen she was writing with. "You say . . . a boy was hit last night? . . . Is he . . . is he . . . ?"

Mrs. Ransom looked at Rilla for a moment before speaking. "Apparently he is still alive, though no one knows the extent of his injuries. He was lifeflighted to Primary Children's Hospital in Salt Lake City last night." She paused. "You seem upset. Did you know him?"

Rilla picked up the pen, but her hand was shaking. "No, no . . . it's just the shock. Such a terrible thing." She set the pen down again. "Do they know . . . who did it?"

"I understand that the police assume it was a passing tourist or an illegal alien, perhaps an unlicensed migrant worker. Any local person would have stopped."

"Why, yes . . . of course. Anyone would." Rilla paused. "Anyone. Uh . . . how old is the boy?"

"I think six or seven. The family has so little money, what with Seth Murdock's recent illness and lack of work. And all those mouths to feed. I wonder how they'll manage." Mrs. Ransom looked at Rilla with some concern. "Say,

Perfecting Amiable

are you all right?" she asked, taking Rilla's elbow. "Let me run you home. You can do this later."

Rilla pulled away. "No, no . . . I'm fine. It's . . . it's this new medication. I'm not used to it yet." She grabbed her shoulder bag and headed for the door. Mrs. Ransom let her go.

Rilla thought she'd never get home. The colonial style mansion on the upper end of Oak Drive seemed to recede as she drove toward it. She was sick and frightened at the same time. Clearly, what she had struck the evening before was not a dog. It was the Murdock boy. By the time Rilla reached home, however, she was a good deal calmer. She realized that it was not her fault, that the boy must have run into her, and that he should not have been out on the streets alone at that hour of the night. His parents were to blame. On pulling her Mercedes into the third of four garage openings, she went immediately to the big SUV. She had to back it out in order to examine the right front bumper and fender. There was a slight dent in the bumper and a minor scratch or two, but that was all. Nothing anybody was likely to notice. She'd have it repaired in Sage.

Much relieved, Rilla returned the vehicle to the garage and closed the door. She didn't recall having been encumbered by an overactive conscience, ever, and her upset over the news of the Murdock boy she attributed mainly to concern over her own liability. Now Herbert, he was different.

Marilyn Arnold

He was supposed to be the cold-hearted businessman whose conscience was kept securely in wraps, but he had a tender side and a strong sense of right and wrong. She blamed this weakness on his upbringing in Amiable, and she sometimes wondered how a man with an overblown conscience came to own a bank. Then and there, Rilla vowed that she would not tell Herbert what had happened. Why, right off he'd march her down to the sheriff. She couldn't have that. She had her image to think of.

Rilla was almost certain that hitting a pedestrian and not stopping was a crime. But what if you didn't know you had hit a person? Maybe she should ask Herbert about some of the finer points of the law. Then again, maybe she shouldn't. He'd want to know why she was asking. Come to think of it, there was her daughter, Fallon, in Chicago. Fallon knew the law backwards and forwards, and she knew how to get guilty people off. Rilla could hear Fallon now. She'd tell Rilla that if there were no witnesses she was safe. "Just keep your mouth shut," she'd say. Fallon took after her mother's side of the family. "But what if the boy dies?" Rilla would ask. "That doesn't change anything," Fallon would reply. Rilla decided that she would say nothing to Fallon.

Rilla did not want to have killed or injured a child. A dog was one thing; a child was quite another. Nonetheless, she was grateful the Murdocks were one of the poorer families in Amiable. People like that were less likely to raise a

Perfecting Amiable

ruckus. Rilla decided then and there that she would discuss the incident with no one. She had always prided herself on her independence, her strength. She liked to think she had what Hemingway called "grace under pressure." Rilla loved that phrase and took strength from it whenever it came to mind. For herself, she offered no assistance to anyone, and she expected no assistance from anyone—other than hired help. Whatever challenge presented itself, she could handle it. Why, then, was she agitated and afraid? Maybe she could convince Herbert to leave on holiday immediately. A change of scenery would help put this incident behind her.

Herbert was late getting home that evening. He had gone straight from work to Rotary meeting where once again the speaker told the tired men who gathered in the banquet room of the Grab Sum Grub that Amiable had a promising future that included a possible raceway and gun club. When Herbert arrived home, there was the usual note from Rilla. According to this one, she had gone to bed early with a headache. Irmita had left cold cuts in the refrigerator if he wanted a snack. Herbert loosened his tie, kicked off his shoes, and sat down to peruse the latest *Wall Street Journal*. At last he arose, stretched, and wandered out onto the back patio. The evening was unusually cool for that time of year, with a breeze coming out of the north. There in a chaise lounge sat his wife, still as a statue, following his movements with her eyes.

"Hey, I thought you were in bed!" he cried.

"I was. I couldn't sleep, so I came out here to get some air."

"What's the trouble? Are you worried about something? Are the kids okay?"

"I haven't heard from them. That's normal." A bat swooped close, and Rilla ducked. "Are there bats in Washington? I don't remember them."

"There are bats everywhere. We don't have a corner on the market."

"If we did, I suppose you'd invest in them."

He chuckled. "I suppose I would. Well, I'm going to turn in. Do you need anything?"

"No, no, I'm fine. Goodnight."

Herbert went off to bed, but Rilla was not fine, of course, not after what had happened. To make matters worse, someone had apparently targeted her for harassment—or possibly even blackmail. She hadn't mentioned it to Herbert, but crushed in her right hand was a strange note which had been slipped inside her front door. That door had never had a tight seal. Rilla found the note lying in the entry hall next to the door after the servants had left for the day. The note did not threaten bodily harm or ask for money, which puzzled Rilla. In fact, it promised treasure if she could unlock the riddle contained in a twisted maxim. The note instructed her to go

Perfecting Amiable

alone to the Carruth house and ponder the saying, then write its meaning for her personally on a piece of paper and leave it at the house. The maxim she was told to ponder read:

WHAT GOES AGROUND COMES UP FOUND.

Rilla was in no mood for games. Was the writer of the note merely toying with her, preparatory to dropping a bombshell or turning her in to the sheriff? Did the writer of the note witness the hit-and-run? After all, the Escalade was not exactly inconspicuous. She had bought it precisely because it was conspicuous.

Rilla went to bed, but knew she would not sleep. Until today, the Murdock family had scarcely been on her radar screen. She was aware that there was a large family in a small house near the town center, and wondered if that was the Murdock place. The inordinate number of children indicated the Murdocks were either Catholics or Mormons. Tipped over tricycles scattered across the dirt driveway, and dolls on the lawn—in concert with uneven blinds at the windows—told Rilla all she needed to know about these people. Prior to this, Rilla wouldn't have given them a thought. Now she couldn't get them out of her mind. Mrs. Ransom said the boy had been flown to a hospital in Salt Lake City. He must have been seriously injured. The family probably had no medical insurance, Rilla reasoned. Their types never did.

Marilyn Arnold

Rilla became angry—with herself for taking her eyes off the road, with the boy for having been in the wrong place at the wrong time, with his parents for letting him run loose, and with the writer of the note for upsetting her all the more. In just one instant, everything had been ruined. She was a murderer! Unable to lie still, Rilla at last arose and retied the waistband of her silk robe. As it happened, the garages and the master bedrooms were at opposite ends of the large two-story house. She could slip out in the sedan without waking the deep-sleeping Herbert. Which is just what she did, steering by moonlight until she reached the corner. Within minutes, she was crunching up the driveway to the Carruth house, lights off, asking herself if she had totally lost her mind, or if it was departing piecemeal, to keep her interest in the process from flagging.

The crickets hushed momentarily when Rilla invaded their territory, then took up their pulsing chorus again. Rilla realized that before that night she had scarcely been aware of their presence. Not surprisingly. When had she ever slept with an open window? Any time she was outside in the evening, she was preoccupied, wasn't she? Ask Herbert. Rilla circled to the far side of the house, to be less visible should headlights from another car point in her direction. It was bumpy going, and she worried for the underside of the Mercedes.

Perfecting Amiable

Rilla knew the Carruth brothers only by reputation, since she had no cause to trade with them and they did not run in bankers' circles. She sat there, in the shadow of their great folly, feeling the magnitude of it with every breath of night air. She had not attended the Great Dividing of the house because sophisticated persons like herself were above lending credence to such spectacles. Rilla would not have been caught dead among the ill-bred gawkers. Why, then, had she come this night? She didn't know. Nor did she have a clue to the meaning she was supposed to find in some far-fetched maxim. "What goes aground comes up found." It was pure gibberish. Here she was, facing possible criminal charges for running over a child and leaving the scene, and she'd been told to come out here and think!? Well, she had come, and she had thought. Now what?

As Rilla contemplated the imposing form of the Carruth house against the midnight sky, she wondered why she had been sent there. What could she possibly learn from those dead brothers and the shabby symbol of their enmity? She had worries enough of her own without dragging someone else's out of the past. Yet, there stood the house, insisting itself into her consciousness. Then, seemingly out of nowhere, the image of the elder Carruths, the parents whom she had seen no more than a dozen times, sprang into her mind. Their countenances, as she saw them now, seemed lined by deep sorrow, the sorrow they must have lived with daily for endless years. "Those boys," Rilla said haughtily, "they never thought of what their feud with each other was costing their parents. They thought only of themselves. They sacrificed their parents on the altar of their pride." She paused to admire her insight, then added. "A little humility might have saved the lot of them."

Rilla sat a long time with a good many thoughts troubling her brain. She was not accustomed to soul-searching, and most certainly, she had never questioned the rightness of anything she had ever done—with the possible exception of marrying Herbert and moving to Amiable. That decision she blamed on youthful naivete and inexperienced hormones. Finally, shuddering a bit with the cooling night air, Rilla turned the ignition key and bumped back to the driveway. Not until she entered the highway did she switch on her headlights.

The next morning when Rilla awoke, she found herself on the sofa in the study. Herbert had gone to work without waking her. Rilla had never been a heavy drinker, but she figured this was what a hangover felt like. Staggering to the phone on Herbert's desk, she called Irmita and Francesca, telling them to take the day off. She couldn't have them finding her like this, nor did she want them underfoot just now. Her mind was in turmoil. What was she to do? A long shower helped clear her head and set the day's agenda. First, she had to know if the Murdock boy had survived.

Perfecting Amiable

Where could she inquire without arousing suspicion? Where else: the Cuts 'n Curls. She would go in on the pretext of buying hair spray—but her primary purpose would be to listen.

Rilla was not disappointed. For sheer news value, a hit-and-run in Amiable rivaled an alien invasion in Los Angeles, where ordinary murder and general mayhem were so common as to receive scant notice. The Ladies League of Amiable, all of whom were loyal customers of Leola Baxter, would rise to the occasion and keep the accident a hot news item for days, perhaps weeks. When Rilla came in, Leola was busily rolling curlers into Carlynn Ingles' hair while Edna Fay Boyack and Elja Nexel looked on. They had come early for their appointments in order to participate in the enlightenment the beauty shop provided—all without extra charge. Rilla scanned the products on every shelf in the establishment, taking her own sweet time to do it. Sometimes the presence of Carlynn Ingles and her well-publicized B.A. degree added a spirit of competition to the conversation. Other times, her presence dampened the enthusiasm of the gossipers. Today was one of the good days.

"I doubt they'll ever ketch 'im," Leola was saying. "He's prolly in Timbuktu by now."

"Unless it was a local done it," Elja said. "A local's gonna let it slip out sometime, and bam! they'll have 'im."

Carlynn Ingles spoke up. "Don't be so sure it was a 'him,' she said. "Women drive cars, too, you know."

A can of hair spray clattered to the floor at Rilla's feet, and all eyes turned in her direction. "Oh!" she cried, "I'm so sorry. I'll buy that one. It slipped out of my hand." Rilla was not accustomed to apologizing for anything, but the words were out before she could yank them back.

Edna Fay chimed in, her eyes still fixed on Rilla. "Well, I hope they throw the book at whoever done it, him or her, hittin' a little boy like that. It's a cryin' shame."

A deep red crept up Rilla's neck into her cheeks. Against her better judgment, she spoke: "No one does something like that on purpose. Whoever did it must feel terrible."

"Well," Edna Fay exclaimed under her breath, "look who's stickin' up fer the criminals!"

"Hush, Edna Fay," Carlynn warned in a low voice, "don't make yourself any enemies you don't need."

"There's too many criminals runnin' around loose, if y' ask me, on account a' them bleedin' heart liberals," Edna Fay retorted.

Leola, ever the diplomat, steered the conversation back. "How's the little boy? Anybody heard?"

Carlynn spoke up. "I stopped over to the house this morning. Loris Murdock is a friend of mine. Her sister's there with the children while Loris and Seth are with Danny in Salt

Perfecting Amiable

Lake. Apparently he has a broken leg and some cracked ribs, along with scrapes and bruises. They expect to bring him home in a day or two. It could have been a lot worse."

Elja spoke up. "I wonder what they're doin' fer money. All those kids, an' him just gettin' over bein' sick and outta work. I guess it's been a slow summer so far in the paintin' business. An' winter'll be even worse. They ought t' move t' Las Vegas where houses are goin' up right'n left all year long."

"Yeah, but if they did that, then they'd have t' live in Las Vegas!" Edna Fay cried. "I'd druther be poor."

"Well, you got your wish," Carlynn said under her breath. "We all did."

Greatly relieved at the news about Danny Murdock, Rilla paid for the offending can of hair spray and left the beauty shop, heading toward home. She was no longer uncertain about where the Murdocks lived because she had looked them up in the telephone directory. Almost unconsciously, she drove by the house and revisited the scene of the accident, careful to show no more than casual interest. The road appeared to be stained a little in the vicinity where Rilla had heard the thud, but she was not about to check it closely. Somebody official might be watching for suspicious activity at the scene of the crime. It occurred to Rilla that she needed to wash the Escalade immediately, to remove any possibly incriminating evidence.

Marilyn Arnold

Then, for some reason, she pulled back onto Main Street and pointed the nose of the Mercedes toward the Carruth place. She couldn't go there in broad daylight, could she? What excuse might she give if someone spotted her? Yet she couldn't seem to stay away. Not only did the proverb and its riddle nag at her incessantly, but the tragedy of the Carruth house returned again and again to her thoughts. It wasn't the deaths of the brothers that bothered her most. It was what lay behind the deaths. She had arrived at a new awareness of the destructive power of selfishness and pride in human lives. The house, she realized now, with insight that surprised her, stood for more than the few lives that struggled and expired there. Teachings from a long-ago literature class came to mind, and she saw the house as a metaphor for the human race, a symbol of love's failure, a microcosm of the broken world. Adorned with such language, the house took on a kind of eloquence in her mind, with mythic implications.

As she pulled into the unkempt Carruth driveway, the bleakness of the physical structure brought her abruptly back to reality. Why, why was I singled out, and by whom? she demanded silently. What have I to do with those sorry Carruths, or anybody else? Annoyed at her own agitation, she stopped the car at the back corner of the house and opened the door, then slammed it closed again. But the earlier thought persisted. Was she really so far wrong in supposing that the mending of a quarrel between two brothers might

166

Perfecting Amiable

have unleashed a healing power in a larger world? If just one brother had swallowed his pride and gone to the other in humility and love, mightn't he have triggered a miracle? "What goes aground comes up found." Perhaps the seemingly senseless riddle was not so senseless after all. "'Aground' could mean something like coming down off your high horse, couldn't it?" Rilla whispered.

Every day for the next several days, Rilla found herself parked at the Carruth house. It wasn't her idea of good time, but it had become something of an obsession. And every day she resisted its promptings; every day she tried to forget that she had struck a boy with her car. In fact, until now, basking in self approval had been Rilla's favorite occupation. It ranked right up there with sneering and finding fault. She had always been quite satisfied with herself, rather relishing her position atop the social ladder in Amiable. She did not fancy going "aground," not even to be "found," or to save her soul, and certainly not to save anyone else's. Not that she had ever considered her soul to be at risk, of course. Rilla had not been a church-goer because she never saw any benefit in it for a person of her station. Religion was for the huddled masses. Nonetheless, her visits to the Carruth house to date had some value because they confirmed her views about the doltish lower classes. She could see plainly where Thoral and Thurlin had gone wrong and what they should have done differently. Self examination? Well, that was another matter entirely. She had enough on her mind without venturing there.

It was an afternoon in mid-July when Rilla visited the Carruth house for what she vowed would be the last time. She had to break its hold on her, even if it meant complying with all the instructions on the original note. But the longer she stared into the vacant eyes of the abandoned house, the more she felt as though the house were studying her instead of the other way around. As though taking instruction, albeit unwillingly, Rilla drew a pen and notepad from her handbag and began to write, slowly, mechanically at first, then faster and faster. Where her predecessors had written comparatively few words, she wrote two pages. When she was finished, Rilla sat back, took a deep breath, and tore the sheets from the lined pad. Glancing around to make certain no one was about, she folded the sheets together twice and walked to the house. There she quickly stuffed them under a loose board that framed a window on the house's far side and hurried back to her car. Then Rilla stopped, turned, took a hesitant step or two toward the house, and turned again. She covered the distance from the house to the highway in record time, and within minutes she was barreling down Main Street toward Oak Drive.

Preoccupied with her own thoughts, she didn't notice the flashing red and yellow lights coming up behind her until she slowed for the turn onto Oak Drive. Her heart leaped into her throat. They know! she cried silently, stopping her

Perfecting Amiable

vehicle. Someone saw me hit the boy! Panic chased out reason, and Rilla was certain she was going to be arrested and charged with the crime she knew she had committed. Her first thought was to bully and intimidate the young deputy who was walking toward her.

"Can I see your driver's license and registration, ma'm?"

Rilla's resolve failed. She came unglued. The sophisticated lady, by her own admission the envy of all the lesser folk, in that instant "lost it," as they say. An overpowering sense of her own guilt washed over her, and suddenly she was spilling out all the pent-up emotion that had been building inside her since the accident. "Yes, yes!" she cried. "I hit him, I hit him and left. I thought he was a dog or a coyote. Suddenly he was in front of me, and I didn't see him, and it was getting dark, and so I hit him." She paused and buried her face in her hands. "Arrest me, I'm guilty."

The astonished officer looked confused. "Who you talkin' about, ma'm?"

"Why, the little Murdock boy! I must have hit him. I felt a thud, but I thought it was some animal. I'm so sorry," she sobbed.

"Oh, him! Why, ma'm, you didn't hit him." The deputy smiled. "We got the guy hit him already. Somebody seen him do it, in his little pickup, after he downed a few beers at Sally's place. He's here workin' on that new piece a' road that's goin' in t'other side a' Lavoid's place."

169

Rilla looked up in disbelief. "Are you sure?"

"Oh, yes ma'm. He confessed and ever'thing. They took a piece a' the boy's shirt off'n his bumper."

"But . . . but I hit something that night."

"Well, maybe it was you hit the boy's big German shepherd when it run out into the street. You couldn't help that, I 'spect, what with it gettin' dark an' all."

Rilla was dazed. "But the boy. How did the boy get hurt?"

"He saw the dog lyin' there an' run to it. He was bendin' over that ol' dog when this fella hit him."

"Then . . . I'm not under arrest?" Rilla sat back trying to process this news. "Then why did you stop me?"

"Just to say your left brake light's burnt out, ma'm." The deputy hesitated. "Oh, an' you were goin' over the speed limit back there, too, but I'll let you off with a warnin' this time."

Rilla shook her head in disbelief. "But . . . but what about the dog? I apparently killed the boy's dog."

The officer smiled. "Well, that's b'tween you'n him, ma'm. I can't arrest you fer that unless you done it on purpose." He turned to leave, then looked back. "You slow down just a bit, y' hear? I don't want t' hafta give you a ticket."

Rilla sat a long time, staring straight ahead, hands locked around the steering wheel. For some reason, she felt lonesome for Herbert and hoped he would be home for supper. She felt as though she had just surfaced, exhausted, after nearly drowning in a huge, dark lake.

Perfecting Amiable

The next morning Rilla set Irmita and Francesca to work polishing silver and cleaning ceiling fans, and she was out the door and off to Sage. Several hours later, she was on her way back to Amiable with a companion, a fluffy German shepherd puppy named Gus. He lay there beside her in the Escalade, sound asleep in his travel cage. He wore a bright red collar and several tags identifying him and his new owner, Master Daniel Murdock. Rilla felt strangely happy. She hadn't felt this way since she was nine years old and her workaholic grandfather turned up unexpectedly at her piano recital. She was to play a simplified version of "The Flower Song," but in her flustered joy she had forgotten the piece. Rilla could still see her grandfather, smiling, walking toward her, sitting beside her and playing the first few bars. She had looked up at him, smiled, and sailed through the piece from start to finish.

That was a long time ago, but you don't forget those blessed moments of pure happiness.

When Loris Murdock answered her knock sometime later, Rilla stammered a little. She had no planned speech.

"Here . . . this is for the boy, . . . Danny, I mean. His name is Gus."

Mrs. Murdock looked at her curiously. "For Danny? Why?" The woman looked tired, but her face was soft and friendly.

"I . . . I think I'm the one who ran over his dog. "I'm so

. . . so sorry. Is he still in the hospital? Are you the aunt?"

"No, no, I'm Danny's mother, Loris Murdock. Would you like to see him?"

"Well . . . would it be all right? Is he . . .?"

"We were lucky. It could have been so much worse. Come in, he's on the sofa." She paused. "You're Mrs. Ingersoll, aren't you?"

"Yes . . . yes, I am. Uh, you can call me Rilla."

She followed Loris Murdock into the small living room, surprised at how comfortable and clean it was despite its modest furnishings. The home felt warm and inviting, like Mrs. Murdock herself.

"Danny, someone's here to see you," his mother said, "and she has something for you."

That was the beginning of a friendship between a boy, a dog, and a middle-aged woman who found herself in the middle of a small miracle. She also found, quite to her surprise, that the Ingersoll mansion was badly in need of painting, inside and out. Seth Murdock was more than happy to take on the project. After that? Well, the Citizens Bank was looking a little shabby, Rilla thought, and could use a new coat of paint. Herbert Ingersoll agreed completely. And, quite mysteriously, the medical bills for Danny's life flight and hospital stay arrived at the Murdock home stamped "paid in full."

Nine

Merland Swollet, "Shy Merland" the Amiable locals called him, sat biting the end of his BIC ballpoint pen at his mother's white enamel kitchen table. It was where he always worked, and the top was marred by indentations in the painted wood where he sometimes pressed too hard with his pen. "Put somethin' under that paper or else let up on that pen," she had told him dozens of times, but he usually forgot. Genius cannot be held hostage to concern for a mere table top. After all, a kitchen table serves just as well with dents as without. In his view, the dents gave his mother's table a certain distinction. He was tempted to autograph it for posterity, in case he ever became famous.

Marilyn Arnold

On this particular day in early August, Merland was working on anniversary poems for his employer, Sweetsap Greeting Cards in St. Louis, Missouri. He had polished off a belated birthday piece and a ditty on friendship, and now he was hung up on the final lines for an anniversary card that would have special appeal for long-term couples. It was his private opinion that long-term relationships were so rare these days that there wasn't much of a market for cards celebrating them, but Sweetsap had insisted. They always did, and Merland always complied. It was when he was struggling for a rhyme that his mother's table suffered the most, what with the scratching out and heavy-handed doodling. This is what he had so far:

> When sorrow touched my life with tears
> And storm clouds gathered 'round my fears,
> You were there.
> When laughter filled our home with joy
> And never harsh words did annoy,
> You were there.

It was the third and final verse that was giving him trouble. What he wanted to say was that when death approaches for the speaker, he or she knows the lifemate will be there. Merland had tentatively settled on a very poetic line, one that reduced a two-syllable word to one. Observation told

Perfecting Amiable

him that true poets did that a lot, to make the words sound fancy instead of ordinary. Their favorites were "e'er" and "ne'er" and "o'er." He tried another line:

When time is spent and life is o'er . . . But he couldn't find a satisfactory line to follow it. He thought of:

And I will never see you more . . . But he thought that confused the issue as to who might be dying—the speaker or the one spoken to. Finally, he settled on the following version, even though he had to give up "o'er" for it, because he was up against a deadline and Sweetsap Greeting Cards would brook no delays:

When I grow old and life is through
And I must bid you fond adieu,
You'll be there.

Merland sighed heavily and handed his mother the final version for typing. He thought maybe "fond adieu" sounded almost as poetic as "o'er," especially for older people. Merland had never learned to type, nor did he own a computer. His mother, Lureene Swollet, prepared his pieces on a manual Royal typewriter, one "pome" as she called them, per page, and he sent them in. Sweetsap paid him fifty dollars per ditty, so the more he wrote, the more money he got.

Marilyn Arnold

His high school English teacher had encouraged him back then to pursue a writing career, perhaps on the premise that shy social misfits can engage the world better through the written word than in person. Or maybe he was one of the few students in her classes who knew the difference between a subject and a verb, even though he had forgotten it now and it didn't seem to matter. At any rate, after high school, on the strength of her praise, he enrolled in the creative writing program offered by Opportunity Knocks, a correspondence school his mother's elderly aunt learned about from a coupon in the Sunday supplement in Phoenix, Arizona.

"Is this the last one?" his mother asked. "I like to do 'em all at once, so's I don't hafta ruin more than one day per batch."

Merland flinched. He knew he should learn to type so as to spare his mother the work and the worry of preparing the final drafts of his poems, especially when a deadline was close. He also knew he should learn to use a computer, but just thinking about it gave him a rash and a persistent cough. "These two more," he said, handing her the verses for belated birthday and friendship cards.

"Hmmph," she responded, and began reading the first one aloud in the exaggerated sing-song manner she adopted when reciting his work:

The years flow swiftly to their fate
And even though my wish is late,

Perfecting Amiable

Just know that in this mortal race
You make the world a better place.

"What's this'n for, a birthday somebody missed?"
Merland hated to hear the commentary that followed his mother's readings. It was a big price to pay for her typing services. He sighed and she went on: "I always said ain't nobody got no business missin' nobody's birthday." As usual, she didn't wait for Merland to respond, but went ahead and slaughtered the other piece:

Some friends desert when going's tough,
Some leave when pathways grow too rough,
But you are constant, ever near,
And always fill my life with cheer.

"Now that's what I call a darned good pome," Lureene exclaimed, slapping the paper with the back of her hand. "It makes me lonesome for your daddy— rest his soul. Your grandmama's gift has showed up in you, d' you know that? She could spiel off a pome at the drop of a hat."
Merland replied that she had so informed him several hundred times. Certainly, the worst part about preparing these little rhymes was that his mother always recited them before she typed them. Thus, he had to endure himself, rendered at full volume and in whatever manufactured emotion

177

Marilyn Arnold

Lureene thought appropriate to the content.

Judging from when he finished high school, people figured Merland was somewhere in his early forties. Being an only child and woefully unskilled in the social graces, Merland had always been afraid of girls. Nothing had changed, except possibly to get worse, what with his premature balding, his round little belly, and his thick horned-rim glasses. It was perhaps inevitable that after his father's death he would wind up back in Amiable with his mother. As a young man, Merland had ventured as far as Sage and taken a job in a Sweetsap retail store. During slow periods, he read cards. The humorous ones were beyond his abilities, but he found himself able to write sentimental verses in the same style as the ones he read. A fellow worker convinced him to send some of his work to Sweetsap. To his surprise, the company bought his ditties, and he became a freelance versifier.

Local folks knew Merland was bashful and backward, but there were things about him they didn't know. For instance, no one but his mother knew about his teddy bear collection, and even she—being denied access to his room— didn't know the full extent of it. He had taken to sneaking new ones in during her nap times and her trips to the Amiable Mercantile, and to various other establishments around town. The bears came by mail order to a post office box, and he hid them in the garage until he could slip them into the house. It

Perfecting Amiable

was getting so he hardly had space for sleeping, what with the teddies of every size and color filling his room. They were a great comfort to him, and with them he was witty and eloquent. Even debonair. That was the word he applied to himself when he conversed with the bears.

He was at his best with them. They required nothing of him but occasional dusting off, and they were good company. Better than his mother because they didn't talk, and he wasn't in their debt. Quite the opposite. He owned them! Merland installed a lock on his bedroom door and carried the key with him at all times. Lureene was offended at first, but she got used to it, telling him she was glad to have him doing his own cleaning these days. Nonetheless, every once in a while she brought up the subject of the bears. Usually, she did this at suppertime, when he was a captive audience. Although Merland could be rather insensitive at times, in general he was a man of few words who would never in a million years stomp away from the table. Especially when he was hungry and his mother had made chili pot pie, his favorite. She always seemed to time her lengthiest teddy bear discourses with the serving of chili pot pie.

"I can't understand it," she'd say, "a grown man playin' with teddy bears!"

"I don't play with them."

"Why, it ain't normal!" she'd add.

"I only look at them."

Marilyn Arnold

"Well, I hear words in there sometimes. An' as for that lock, you might's well take it off. I wouldn't go in that room a' yours for love nor money. One a' these days you're gonna suffocate t' death in there with all that fluff an' stuffing. An' don't come cryin' t' me when you do. I'll say I told you so. An' don't think I'm buryin' you with none a' them animals, neither. I'm givin' the whole kit and kaboodle t' the county for the homeless children an' such like."

"There's no way you'll live longer than I do."

"We'll see, we'll just see. B'sides, you better pray I live a long time. Who'd type your pomes if I wasn't here t' do it?"

Clearly, Merland's mother viewed this as her clinching argument, and she always ended with it. Sometimes, however, she'd add a little kicker: "Put that in your pipe and smoke it," she'd say.

Merland's excursions from home were mainly to the post office, a small white stucco building two doors down from the town offices. He had two purposes in going, one to mail his greeting card rhymes off to Sweetsap and the other to collect his teddy bears. On the particular day in question, Merland rushed to get his last batch of poems off before deadline. It was against his principles to pay the extra charge for one- or two-day delivery, and he would never consider the extravagance of sending by Federal Express, so he was forever in a dither. His mother always said procrastination

Perfecting Amiable

was his middle name. It was the only five-syllable word in her vocabulary. Her modus operandi was to wrap every complex issue in a cliché, as if that settled the matter. Which it did—for her. It drove Merland crazy.

The lifestyle Merland had chosen for himself, and imposed on his mother, pretty much meant that, except for his teddy bears, there were only two people in his life—his mother, Lureene Swollet, and the postmistress, Nola Bell Pulley. Nola Bell had moved to Amiable some twenty years ago, when Merland was in Sage. She came from a small town in Colorado to run the Amiable post office pretty much single-handed, except for the two men who served as sorters and carriers. If she was sick or on vacation, one of them took over for her, and they did the same for each other. If two of them were sick, they called in Arlo Blanchard, who had been trained as a backup.

No one knew for certain how old Nola Bell was, but the guesses ranged from forty to fifty. She was young when she arrived, everybody knew that, so young that at first some people refused to trust her with their mail. For example, in the beginning, Rilla Ingersoll took her important mail to Sage, and LaDessa Payton gave hers to the carrier and asked him to see to it personally. But gradually people came to have confidence in Nola Bell, and she became a fixture in Amiable life. So much a fixture that she hardly existed as a person in the minds of the citizenry. She was only the postmistress. No one thought to invite her to private social gatherings, or to inquire of her family back in Colorado whom she visited once a year.

Indeed, Nola Bell was no beauty. Her blonde hair was permed in tight curls all over her head, and she couldn't seem to get her eyebrows or her lipstick on straight. But except for that, and a little unobtrusive pudginess, one could scarcely fault her. She ran the post office efficiently and almost never misplaced mail. It's true, she could become a little absent-minded when Merland Swollet came in to pick up a package or to mail a batch of verses off to Sweetsap Greeting Cards in St. Louis. Merland never said a word more than was necessary to her, and sometimes he didn't say anything at all. Nola Bell could smile and try to strike up a conversation, but mostly Merland just said "Ummm" or "Unnh." For a poet, he seemed astonishingly short of words. The more naive folks in Amiable concluded that he used up all his words in writing and had none to spare for people. The less naive had other opinions. Nola Bell was of the former, more kindly group.

Everyone knew what Merland did for a living. His mother made sure of that. After all, how many bona fide paid poets were there in Amiable, anyway? Merland was the only resident with that claim to fame, and given the inclinations of the current crop of Amiable school children, he wasn't

Perfecting Amiable

likely to have much competition any time soon. Lucky for
him he didn't try to make his mark in video games. Yes,
everyone knew what Merland did for a living, but they did-
n't know what he did for pleasure. They didn't know about
the teddy bears. That was not the sort of thing a mother, no
matter how talkative she was, would share with her associ-
ates at the beauty parlor or the Ladies League. Oh, no. In
public, her lips were buttoned on that subject, all right.

But that still left a possible loophole. Nola Bell Pulley
and her co-workers at the post office. Merland was pretty
sure the men wouldn't take the trouble to read the small
print identifying the mail order firm that sent his teddy
bears. Even the little bear insignia behind the name didn't
seem to raise any questions with them—or he'd have heard
about it. After all, the wives of those men patronized the
Cuts 'n Curls. The beauty shop was the reason Amiable did-
n't need a radio station. But Nola Bell? She had noticed the
bear insignia and asked him about it once. He had only
grunted and walked out with his package. Many a time he
wished he didn't have to ask Nola Bell for the packages that
wouldn't fit in his small post office box.

On the day Merland was rushing to get his manilla envelope of verses mailed before the truck left, he was not the
only patron lined up at Nola Bell's counter. In front of him
was the mother of the little boy that was run over—

183

Murdock, was it?—and behind him was that Ransom woman he had seen a few times over the last several years. He didn't know much about her except that his mother said she was an odd sort of woman and a busybody. As they waited together, she tried to strike up a conversation with him, but he kept his eyes lowered and responded with an unintelligible grunt. When he arrived at the counter with his package, Nola Bell smiled brightly.

"Off to St. Louis with this as usual?" she asked. "Oh, how I wish I could write poetry!" Then she blushed and giggled a little. "It must be lovely to be so talented. Might I read some of your poems sometime?" Nola's hands seemed to shake a little as she took Merland's money and carefully placed the postage sticker in the upper right hand corner of the large envelope.

"Hmmph. I dunno. Gotta go." Merland nearly knocked Mrs. Ransom over in his rush to get out of the post office.

Outside he breathed a sigh of relief. Nola Bell made him nervous. So did Mrs. Ransom and just about everybody else in town. He was so nervous he forgot to check his box. Very likely it contained a slip serving notice that his new teddy had arrived, a two-foot panda with a pedigree and a name he couldn't pronounce. Well, it would have to wait; he wasn't going back in there. It was two days before Merland worked up the nerve and the strength to return to the post office for his panda. Getting a batch of poems ready and off to

184

Perfecting Amiable

Sweetsap was such a strain that he often took to his bed for a day or two in a state his mother termed "writer's meltdown." He himself referred to it privately as postpartum depression. He accepted the fact that poets were notorious for their delicate constitutions.

Grateful to see that Nola Bell was serving a patron when he walked into the post office two days later, Merland virtually tip-toed to his box. Unfortunately, it contained no slip about a package, but something else was there, a small envelope addressed to him. Eager to exit the post office while Nola Bell was still occupied, Merland stuffed the envelope in his pants pocket and scurried out the door. Since virtually all the household mail, except from Sweetsap, came courtesy of the mail carrier and was addressed to Lureene Swollet (or possibly Lorraine Swallow, or Louine Smalley, or Louanne Swillet), Merland felt a tiny surge of excitement at seeing his name handwritten on a small envelope. There was no return address. Ripping the envelope open, he began to read the odd words printed in odder still capital letters.

Someone was trying to pull his chain, as Lureene would say. It crossed his mind that the sender was his mother, although the handwriting on the envelope only vaguely resembled hers. "If she can't get my attention one way, she'll try another," he muttered aloud. Indeed, she was a note-sender from the word go. At least two or three times a week, especially if he wasn't around or was locked in his room, she slipped notes under his door. "Don't forget it's garbage day tomorrow," she might say.

Taking the trash can to the street was his job, though he regarded it as an imposition on his artistic soul. She said it was the least he could do to earn his keep.

Other times she would write, "When are you going to change that shirt? It smells."

This habit of his mother's was just another of the things that drove him crazy. As Merland read on, however, it became clear the note inside the envelope was not his mother's. For one thing, she rarely printed, and besides, she was not likely to spend a stamp in order to instruct her son when she had rural free delivery down the hall. Furthermore, puzzles and riddles were not her line. Direct and to the point was her line.

Apparently puzzles and riddles were the name of this particular game. Here was a note from some nut telling him to get himself over to the Carruth house, privately, and ponder this ridiculous statement for its significant application to himself:

STRIKE WHILE THE IRE IS NOT.

The note promised that if he would do what it said, a great treasure would be his. When he had learned something from so pondering, he was to write it on a piece of paper and secure it somewhere at the Carruth house. It was a joke,

Perfecting Amiable

Merland decided, a sick, miserable joke. The one time he got a real letter in the mail, from a person instead of a company, it was a joke. Well, he intended to ignore it.

Merland had no car of his own. He saw no need because his mother had a 1990 Pontiac he could use in an emergency. In the main, he got about on a faded silver motor scooter which he figured used about a quart of fuel a week. "There goes Shy Merland," people would say when he made his trips to the post office.

He didn't want to go to the Carruth place, and he didn't want anybody to spot him heading out there. Still, the thing bothered him. Even his teddy bears gave no comfort. Finally, after two days of pacing back and forth among the blank looks and silent mouths of the bears, he stalked through the kitchen and out the back door. Lureene was right behind him.

"Where you goin'?" she demanded. "You can't take the car 'cause I got to have it this afternoon."

"I'm taking my scooter," Merland called back.

"Stop a minute. You ain't goin' t' the post office t'day, are you? Come in here and let me take your temp'ature. You been actin' strange lately. You comin' down with the quinsy or somethin'?"

Without turning, he waved off her question. "Maybe I'm coming down with infectious mother-itis," he mumbled.

Within minutes he was at the driveway to the Carruth house. Meeting a car approaching from the other direction,

Marilyn Arnold

Merland rode on past the half-house. He wished the house had a less conspicuous entry, or that he had waited until evening. Questions plagued him—why, why, why? Why him? Why riddles? Why this house. Why now? And most of all, who? Who was tempting him into this foolish game? Who had it in for him? Who wanted to watch him suffer? And then there was that foolish adage, a play on the old proverb. "Strike while the ire is not." What was that supposed to mean? Whose ire? When might it come? So he was supposed to "strike," meaning do what? And, as puzzling as anything else: why the Carruth house?

Merland made a U-turn and once more approached the Carruth driveway. Gunning the scooter, he raced over the bumpy ground and parked behind the shed, out of sight from the road. Then he dismounted and perched on an old wooden crate near a struggling box elder tree. The crate gave him a good view of the back of the house, from which angle the house almost appeared whole. The scars from the saw weren't visible, and the foundation was intact. An unexpected wave of sadness swept over him. He tried to remember the house as it was once, before two brothers became enemies. There was a time when the ire was not, he said to himself. There must have been love in that house once. Why did they let it go? Why were selfishness and distrust allowed to drive it out?

And then he began to think how life must have been in that house after love vanished. "Ire . . . ," he said aloud. "Ire

Perfecting Amiable

is the opposite of love. Where ire is, love cannot thrive. And where love is, ire is forbidden. 'Strike while love still exists,' that's what the maxim says." Merland felt a sudden need for his teddy bears, for the comfort they brought. He could never be hurt by them. They could never disappoint him. They could never make demands. And then it hit him. They could never love him, either, nor could he truly love them except superficially, the way one might be said to "love" ice cream. That kind of love meant nothing, being synonymous only with pleasure. Was he as bad as the Carruth brothers, who valued something inanimate above each other and above their parents? They fed on anger and pride, while he himself fed on fear—fear of giving love, fear of what it might require of him.

Merland sat a long time on that crate. In fact, it was dark when he slowly puttered down the driveway. He knew no one loved him, with the possible exception of his mother because mothers love their children, whether they deserve love or not. He wasn't even sure that he loved her. It was not something he had ever thought about, not even on Mother's Day, though he wrote sweet lovey-dovey verses by the hundred. And none more lovey-dovey than for the mothers of the world. What did he know about the subject after all?

All that night he lay on his bed, his teddy bears heaped around him, hungering for whatever it was others seemed to have found, or to have missed, or to have thrown away. How did it come? Was it too late for him? He wept bitter tears that night, and by morning he had come to a decision.

At mid-morning his mother started off to the Ladies League brunch featuring a guest speaker from the Sage City Yoga and Belly Dancing Club. Of all this she informed him by hollering through his locked door. They were both accustomed to this form of communication. As soon as Lureene had left the premises, Merland hopped on his scooter and headed for the Amiable Mercantile, which happened to own a large utility van. He arranged with Weldon Tray to lease the Merc's van for a day. It was a rather different driving experience from operating his motor scooter, but he crushed only two of his mother's peony bushes backing it up her driveway. He lined the van with a sheet from his bed and began gently stacking his teddy bears in the vehicle.

At first, he thought he was going to cry, but then, the more teddies he loaded, the lighter his heart began to feel. In fact, by the time he had lifted the last bear from its place on his window sill, he was humming a song his mother used to sing when he was a boy, "Give, said the little stream, give oh give." Merland walked out his bedroom door, leaving it wide open. He placed the last bear, a brown one in a space suit, in the van, took the key to his bedroom door out of his pocket and threw it as far as he could into the vacant lot next door. In less than two hours, Merland was pulling up in front of the child and family services building in Sage.

Perfecting Amiable

Re-entering Amiable later that day, Merland slowed when he neared the Carruth house, giving a smart salute as he passed. His essay was ready, folded up in his shirt pocket. Before long, the poet laureate of Amiable had returned the van and was steering his motor scooter once more into the driveway of the divided house. He parked in plain sight and walked over to the house. Then, he ceremoniously removed a small candle from his pants pocket, lit it, and dripped wax on his folded message to seal it. That done, he walked three times around the house, tucked his missive under a crack in the siding, bowed at the back door, mounted his scooter, and drove home.

"Now I know yer sick," Lureene Swollet said to Merland when he walked in the house all smiles.

"No," he answered, "for the first time in my life I'm not sick. I've been sick a long time."

His mother looked at him. "That ain't so. Maybe a little under the weather lately, is all. Rest of the time you've been healthy, 'cept for when you've got a deadline an' you've put it off. An' then you're mostly just ornery and pale. Not what I'd call sick sick, just sorta peak-ed."

"How'd you like to go down to Sally's, right now, for a bite to eat—on me?"

Lureene looked at him in disbelief. "Now I know you're sick." She smiled at him. "Let's go b'fore you recover."

191

Marilyn Arnold

A day or two later, Merland remembered the panda teddy that was hung up in the postal system somewhere, probably the holding box in Amiable by now. He could give it to his mother, but she'd think it foolishness. Well, he'd better pick it up in any case. Sure enough, there in his otherwise empty post office box was a slip indicating that an oversized package was being held for him. He presented the slip to Nola Bell and she disappeared for a few moments. He took the package to the patrons' work counter and used a key to slice through the packing tape. Behind the counter, he could feel Nola Bell's eyes on him and his package. This is the first time he had opened a bear in the post office. Luckily the office was empty of customers.

Oh, this panda was a honey and had the sweetest face he had ever seen on a teddy bear. Merland hesitated only a split second, though. Then he turned and walked back to Nola Bell at the counter.

"For . . . for you," he said, handing her the panda.

Tears came to her eyes. "For me? But . . . but, why?" she stammered.

"Because . . . just because. No reason." Merland studied his shoes intently. "Uh, could I maybe . . . uh, come by this evening? I've, uh, got some new poems to write. Maybe, uh . . . maybe you could give me some ideas? You know . . . inspire me?"

"Well, I don't know how inspiring I am, but I maybe could try . . . I sure could try."

Ten

It was August, and as the afternoon wore on, Leoma Hamaker Blinn sat contemplating life from the window of room 302 in the Amiable Hotel. She still couldn't believe she was here when she had a home of her own less than a mile away—and a husband. Why was she in the hotel? Well, it's a long story, a story with its origin in the fact that she had settled for Archie Blinn when everybody knew she could have done better. Everybody being principally Leoma's mother, LaPrele Victoria Hamaker, and Leoma herself. She had done the settling some thirty-five years ago, after she came back to Amiable from finishing school where she mainly learned to put on makeup and airs.

Marilyn Arnold

The local boys, unfinished all, could not hold a candle to the "men" she had dated, or aspired to date, during her brief tenure in the East. The East in this case being Denver, where her maternal grandmother once had connections. Leoma had been a pretty girl, with brown hair and good skin and teeth. Now, of course, dye was required to keep color in her hair, and her skin had loosened along with several of her teeth. Nonetheless, she still bore the remnants of her finishing school training. She knew how to set a table and fold a napkin, even if no one else cared a whit.

In order to survive, a woman consigned to life in Amiable as the wife of the local barber pretty much had to abandon any illusions of grandeur she might have entertained while handicapped by the vanities of youth. If she had married a man of means, she might have qualified to associate with Rilla Rowberry Ingersoll. Things being what they were, however, Leoma clung to her manners and expectations, and to her view of herself as an icon of gracious living in a culturally challenged town. In her clinging she was aided and abetted by her now eighty-five-year-old mother, LaPrele, who had lived with Leoma and Archie for a few years after Leoma's father died but had since opted for an assisted living facility in Sage.

It was no mystery to Leoma why her mother moved out, though it did hurt her feelings. No octogenarian in her right

Perfecting Amiable

mind would want to live in a home where if the owners had installed a revolving door, most of the occupants would have been better served. In other words, transient traffic was heavy in the Blinn household. It wasn't that the good-natured Archie minded having LaPrele there. Not at all. The trouble was, he didn't mind having anybody there if that person had what he considered a legitimate claim on his hospitality. As Leoma always said, in Archie's book anyone still on this side of the grave automatically qualified. Only the dead were unwelcome. Archie didn't put a limit on the number, either. What was one more in a house he managed to keep filled with strays most of the time?

Leoma had borne no children of her own, and as time passed perhaps Archie felt obligated to fill in the blanks and empty beds with any Tom, Dick, or Harry who happened along—especially if that Tom, Dick, or Harry was related to him. Then, too, with her mother at the threshold of her second childhood, Leoma was gaining some firsthand experience in parenting. But it was the people Archie brought home for her to feed, clothe, and house that made her wish for a different life. What had happened to her ethereal finishing school dreams? Why was she stuck where her charms went largely unnoticed and unappreciated—were, in fact, a liability? These were the questions with which Leoma was entertaining herself in room 302 of the Amiable hotel that sultry August day.

Marilyn Arnold

Oh, during the early years of her marriage, before she and Archie were discovered by the loose nuts on his family tree, Leoma had offered little classes in her home for small girls whose mothers thought their daughters could profit from an introduction to grace and manners, and Leoma was a person who was reputed to have some of both. But she didn't have to feed those small girls, and clean up after them, and listen to their wild ideas all day long. She could teach them to walk with a book balanced on their heads and to place forks at the left of the plates, but she wasn't required to love them. She could tell them stories about her exciting romances, and about dancing with princes—well, practically princes—while at finishing school. She could tell them about attending *La Traviata* with Spencer Bloomfield and being pursued by other handsome young men. She could tell them about the gala at the Colorado State Capitol. They didn't have to know it was all invention. Any more, she wasn't so sure it was invention. Would all the details be so clear in her mind if she hadn't been there?

Archie was a man with a big heart, maybe too big. If it was possible to be generous to a fault, that's what Archie was. He failed to realize that Leoma had worries enough of her own, that the last thing she needed was an endless string of drifters under her roof. She had begun to resent his welcoming anybody and everybody and then going blissfully off to

Perfecting Amiable

his barbershop, though she did concede that he had to stand on his feet long hours every day to keep everybody fed. Throughout the day, naturally, it was Leoma who was stuck with Archie's charity cases. As she sat in her hotel room thinking things through, Leoma knew that sometimes she had only one or two extras on the dinner wagon. But even so, these "guests" were not people a civilized person could enjoy. They slurped and burped their way through meals, never using the proper fork or spoon, tucking their cloth napkins at their throats or blowing their noses in them, talking with their mouths full, and doing every other thing strictly forbidden at Miss Brenda Lawrence's Finishing School.

When Leoma married Archie Blinn, she had been grateful enough not to end up an old maid, but she had not known his family. He had discovered Amiable on a fishing trip with friends, liked the area, and decided to settle down. Shortly after his arrival the young bachelor saw Leoma walk past the hotel where he was cutting hair and shining shoes. He claimed it was love at first sight, and the rest, as they say, is history. Before long, he saved enough money to acquire his own little shop, and the two of them found a suitable house to call their own. Soon enough, however, Leoma learned that Archie was the only bright light in a whole rack of dim bulbs, and that over time many of those dim bulbs, and some of their even dimmer offspring, would appear on her doorstep.

Marilyn Arnold

As she stared at the street outside her hotel window, Leoma could see them, in something like a parade of the grotesque, landing in her spare rooms, taking space in her life and her refrigerator. She remembered Kendell's arrival as though it were yesterday. Kendell was the fifteen-year-old son of Archie's younger brother, Wendell Bruce, who had joined up with a colony of polygamists on the Utah-Arizona border. Kendell was born to Wendell Bruce's third wife. Leoma figured they had trouble coming up with new names for so many children, so they just did variations on ones already in use. In any case, Kendell had problems that had nothing to do with his name. One of them was that as his father Wendell grew older, he acquired a taste for younger and younger women. Wendell Bruce had therefore taken on additional wives since Kendell's birth and was fathering children right and left, more or less losing Kendell in the shuffle.

When Wendell Bruce called to ask Archie if he and Leoma could take Kendell in for a while, Archie, true to form, said sure. Naturally, Archie had to go get the boy, and he found the return trip to Amiable—which he described to Leoma as a monologue before a fence post—less rewarding than the trip out. Archie entertained himself by talking a blue streak about how good the Amiable high school was, and how much Kendell would love it, and how much fun they would have fishing on weekends. The boy's participation consisted of an occasional bored grunt from where he

Perfecting Amiable

slumped in the passenger seat biting his fingernails and smelling as though he worked in a fish cannery.

This was before Leoma's mother, LaPrele, moved in with them and then out again, and just after Archie's cousin Baxter and his nine-year-old son had left, two steps ahead of the law. Archie had not known until Baxter and the boy departed that the boy's mother had legal custody of him. Furthermore, father and son were featured on one of those "have you seen us?" cards that come out in the mail every week, a fact that gratified Baxter no end. Leoma protested that she needed time to recover from the Baxter invasion before she took in anybody else, but Archie only said, "Don't worry, it'll be okay." That's what he always said. "That's easy for you to say," is how she always answered—because it was.

There was Kendell, slouching through the back door, bringing the essence of fish cannery into Leoma's newly scrubbed kitchen.

"So, how was the trip?" she asked with false enthusiasm, but she did not extend her carefully manicured hand. "I'm Aunt Leoma. Uncle Archie will show you to your room downstairs."

Archie looked up in surprise. "Downstairs?"

Leoma gave him one of her don't-you-dare-go-there looks and said through a strained smile, "Why, yes, dear. Kendell will be much more comfortable there, won't you

Marilyn Arnold

Kendell? I swear it's the best bed in the house. Why, I'd sleep there myself if it weren't for the stairs." She chuckled nervously. "Besides, mother could be arriving any day now, and I must keep the upstairs guest room for her."

Kendell's eyes remained glued to the floor. The long sleeves of his wrinkled flannel shirt covered his hands, and his straight dark hair hung forward, covering most of his face. Leoma spoke again, silence in the presence of a sulking fifteen-year-old being a trial for a woman trained in gracious living.

"Well, dinner will be served in about forty-five minutes. I hope you like rhubarb."

Kendell glanced up. "Rhubarb? Whut's that? Ain't it poison?"

Leoma forced a smile. "Why no, it's very good, isn't it, Archie?"

"The best!" Archie agreed. "Now let's get you to your quarters. Follow me."

Leoma always regarded Kendell as one of her failures. She didn't like to fail at anything, not even at partial rehabilitation of someone who didn't deserve to be given the time of day. And that was Kendell. He was a grump the whole eighteen months he was with them. Maybe Archie saw him smile, but she sure didn't. His teachers said he didn't fit in at school and he was always getting in fights. Now

Perfecting Amiable

Archie, he thought the boy was all right, maybe because Archie was a talker and didn't particularly care if the boy opened his mouth to utter a civil word once in a blue moon. But then, Archie saw good in everybody. It was his nature, and it drove Leoma crazy. Why, he wouldn't even listen to the gossip she picked up at the Cuts 'n Curls, and he orchestrated the conversation at the barber shop, so it rarely got out of hand or too personal.

Finally, Kendell said he wanted to go home. Archie tried to talk him out of it while Leoma sat there on pins and needles, but Kendell, God bless him, wouldn't budge. It was a great relief to Leoma, and she didn't even mind having to fumigate the downstairs bedroom and bath because it meant she was rid of the boy. The only trouble was, when Kendell was gone, cousin Baxter came back. Baxter's ex-wife had been so pleased to have her son returned, and Baxter had been so effusively repentant, that she didn't press charges. All the Blinns have a gift for gab. "If they didn't, would I have been persuaded to marry Archie?" Leoma asked herself. Naturally Baxter didn't have a job. He blamed it on the fact that he had been on the run with his nine-year-old and hadn't been able to hone his skills and turn his luck. He needed a place to stay until he could overcome his fatherly grief and find another wife to support him.

Marilyn Arnold

Leoma had scarcely got the clean linens on the down-stairs bed when the doorbell rang and there was Baxter, grinning to beat the band, wearing several days' worth of beard and army fatigues. Though he was supposed to be grieving, he was clearly happy to be back to free room and board in Amiable. Beside Baxter was a tattered canvas duffel that contained all his worldly possessions except his big mongrel dog, Fred. Fred sat there madly slapping his tail on the wooden slats of Leoma's front porch and grinning as broadly as Baxter. He was also drooling freely on Leoma's freshly scoured door mat.

"You can smile again, I'm back!" Baxter beamed, his broken front tooth seeming more noticeable than ever.

"Back for what?" Leoma asked, not smiling even a little.

"Why, for a little family conviviality," Baxter said. "I've missed my favorite cousin and his pretty wife."

Leoma took his comment for what it was, butter-up and flattery. "What's that?" she demanded, scowling at Fred. Baxter had not brought his dog the last time—only his abducted son.

"Why, that's man's best friend, my faithful dog, Fred. "In time, you'll grow to love him as much as I do."

"In a very short time, he'll be out of here and you with him," Leoma said, knowing full well that she was violating the Miss Brenda Lawrence rules of hospitality and that Archie would have been mortified to hear her. "I thought

Perfecting Amiable

you were going to jail," she added drily.

"Why, they let me off, seeing how harmless I am and what a good father I was to the boy. I convinced the authorities, and my wife, that I was driven temporarily insane by lonesomeness for the boy." He looked down at Fred. "But now that I've got me a dog I won't be so lonesome. I also told them I was headed to Amiable where I had a home with a loving cousin and his beautiful wife. So here I am, practically by court order."

"I see. Well, now, you just park yourself here on the porch until Archie comes home, and then we'll see what's to be done with you."

"Fred, here, he's a good house dog. He'll keep the mice out."

"Fred, there, will not set one paw inside my house." Leoma hesitated. "I'll bring you a sandwich, which you can eat out here while you wait for Archie."

As it turned out, what was to be done with Baxter and Fred was that they took up residence in the downstairs bedroom recently vacated by young Kendell. Theoretically, Fred was to come in only during inclement weather, but in fact, Fred slept indoors every night—theoretically on the floor and not the bed. Leoma survived by staying out of the basement for the six months it took Baxter to woo and win Selma Ann Jones who clerked at the Amiable Mercantile. Selma

Marilyn Arnold

Ann had a small home and an inheritance which, with her salary at the Merc, left Baxter free to practice his chosen profession of social and political philosophy, in the park when weather permitted, and in Archie's barbershop when it didn't.

Baxter and Fred weren't the last of what Leoma called the Blinn dross. The only letup was when LaPrele came back, and that was no picnic either. And since she was Leoma's mother and not a Blinn, Leoma could not complain. LaPrele's tenure was rather lengthy, too, but at least there was only one of her. She stayed only three weeks after the next Blinn showed up, however, and then she was off to assisted living. Leoma sometimes wished she had gone with her mother. Sitting there in the hotel, knowing that everyone in town was probably aware by now that she had walked out on Archie, Leoma still felt justified, if not wholly virtuous. She had put up with more than any Christian woman should have to endure. Even the Good Samaritan didn't have to live with the likes of Archie's relatives. He had the right idea. He put the stricken man up at an inn and went his way. Leoma decided that charity has its limits, and if it doesn't, it should.

The trouble is, Leoma reflected, she wasn't happy now either. She missed Archie. When she got to missing Archie too much, it helped to remember others that he had moved in on her. Kendell and Baxter were bad enough, but they

Perfecting Amiable

couldn't hold a candle to Geraldine Muncie, Archie's youngest half-sister, and her two daughters, ages seven and nine. Their names were Trinity and Easter, which, considering the urchins the names were attached to, seemed close to blasphemy in Leoma's view.

It was the arrival of that trio in Amiable, via Greyhound bus, that sent LaPrele Victoria Hamaker fleeing to assisted living. LaPrele was in the guest room at the time, one of two bedrooms upstairs. Archie said, in front of Geraldine and her youngsters mind you, leaving Leoma helpless to do anything but concur, that the downstairs bedroom was too small for three people. Therefore, he and Leoma would move downstairs and give the Muncies their bedroom. No matter that LaPrele would be left to share the upstairs, including the bath, with the Muncies. Only the newer, larger homes in Amiable had two bathrooms on the main floor. The situation was complicated further by the fact that if LaPrele needed help during the night, Leoma would have to climb those stairs to attend to her mother. Luckily, LaPrele's room was above the basement bedroom, and if she banged on the floor Leoma could hear her. From the way he extended courtesies right and left one would think it was Archie, not Leoma, who had graduated from finishing school. Geraldine didn't even seem to notice when LaPrele moved out.

Marilyn Arnold

Sitting in the Amiable hotel filing her nails, Leoma could see better why they called some institutions finishing schools: attempting to follow their precepts in real life could finish a person off. The Muncies stayed six months, and Leoma still swears those were the worst six months of her life. And that was going some because she had a lot of bad months. Archie had warned Leoma against asking what became of Geraldine's husband, and Geraldine never volunteered the information, so that remained a mystery. Geraldine home-schooled the girls year 'round, in Leoma's living room, but she didn't teach what anybody would call a regular curriculum. Leoma wondered how on earth Geraldine decided what to teach, and how on earth Trinity and Easter could pass standardized tests, or even function in the world, after a steady diet of Muncie education.

Of course, there were no textbooks. The girls learned reading and writing mainly from the advertising circulars that came in Leoma's mail. Thus, the words they knew best were words like "sale," and "offer expires," and "easy credit." The rest of their education came from what Geraldine called the book of life. Her life, mainly, and her passing interests. That program was better than nothing, Leoma supposed, but would still seriously handicap any child, even one not already handicapped by being born a Muncie.

For example, Geraldine's passion at the time she moved in with Leoma and Archie was house paint. The first thing

Perfecting Amiable

she said when she walked in the front door was not where's the bathroom, or where do we sleep, but, "Are these walls painted with a latex-based paint" and "is this the best satin finish you could find? Doesn't look like it to me." The paint fervor lasted about three weeks, until Geraldine had exhausted the limited resources available in the paint department at the Amiable Mercantile. During those three weeks, however, the girls were required to memorize the colors on approximately 100 different paint chips, not to mention the relative merits of varnish vs. stain.

Geraldine tested the girls orally and went on to her next craze, the nutrition and longevity of rabbits. Coral Watters at the library had only two non-fiction books that said much of anything about rabbits, and Geraldine didn't think to ask her to check the internet. Leoma and Archie had never invested in a computer, so they were no help. Geraldine, who was a hands-on sort of person, supplemented what little she gleaned from the two books by borrowing two live traps from one of Archie's patrons. She baited them with greens and managed to snare two cottontails.

She and the girls then put one rabbit, the control group, on a liquid diet of sugar water. It was her version of a placebo, based on the glucose IV model. The other, the test group, she fed a diet of canned salmon and lemons. Geraldine's theory argued that there was some kind of nutritional magic in food that ended in the same syllable, in this case "-mon." That this theory would not hold up in languages other than English did not occur to Geraldine. During an appropriate period of observation, she and the girls compared the relative health of the two animals. Of course, the rabbit on sugar water soon died of starvation. The rabbit on salmon and lemons lasted longer, but not much. He didn't seem to have much appetite. It was all right, though, because by the time the rabbits died, Geraldine had moved on to her next enthusiasm—nails.

When the rabbits went to their reward, Leoma had just about reached the end of her patience with Geraldine and her odd notions about the education of children. One day Leoma walked in as Geraldine and the girls squatted on the living room rug around a huge assortment of nails.

"There's a nail for every purpose," Geraldine was saying, "and we are going to learn which nail is for what. See this chart girls? Memorize the pictures."

Trinity and Easter sat there, staring first at the chart and then at the nails.

"It's too hard!" Trinity wailed.

"Yeah, too hard!" Easter echoed.

Out of deference to Archie, Leoma had held her tongue through the paint and rabbit episodes, but she could hold it no longer.

"My word, Geraldine, what are you teaching these children? What child needs to know about nails?"

Perfecting Amiable

"I don't want my children going into the world ignorant of the practical aspects of life," Geraldine replied. Geraldine was a rather skinny woman, and she always looked as if she were in somebody else's clothes—which she probably was. She called the way she and the girls subsisted "living off the land." She was one who firmly believed in charity, especially as others practiced it in her behalf.

"These girls need to be in a regular school," Leoma insisted.

"I teach them what they can't get in school," Geraldine said. "What teacher would take my girls to a hardware store or a garbage dump?"

"Not one in her right mind," Leoma muttered walking toward the door. "Don't you leave a single nail on that rug to ruin my Hoover," she said.

Several weeks later, Geraldine's husband showed up out of nowhere in an ancient Plymouth Voyager, loaded the girls and their mother in the van, and off they went. Leoma gave thanks, and she and Archie reclaimed their bedroom. If only the Muncies had been the last, Leoma might have made it. The one that finally pushed her over the edge was Uncle Clin. He showed up in late June this year, fully expecting to find LaPrele there, pining for company and susceptible to his charms. Obviously, his information was seriously outdated. It would seem he thought wooing and winning the elderly mother of his hostess would give him a more persuasive claim to permanent residency with Archie and Leoma. As Archie explained it, Clin was not exactly Archie's uncle, though he was close enough that Archie did not care to dispute the title. He was a brother-in-law to Archie's father's sister's husband. There was not a drop of Blinn blood in him, though from the way he looked and behaved nobody could tell it. He could have passed for a Blinn on any test except DNA, lie detector included. Scruffy was probably the best word for him, from his unkempt thinning hair to his striped overalls and work boots.

Naturally, Uncle Clin could not be put in the downstairs room because a man of his advanced age (whatever it was) could not be expected to descend and climb stairs on a regular basis. That meant he also shared a bathroom with Leoma and Archie—initially. That arrangement lasted a week, at the end of which Archie and Leoma again moved downstairs and left Clin in sole possession of the upstairs bathroom. From then on it was one unacceptable incident after another. Discovering live trout in the bathtub nearly sent Leoma into orbit, especially since that revelation came the same day she learned Clin slept with his boots on, in her 200 thread count sheets. She also found her best paring knife in Clin's bathroom, covered with whiskers and shaving cream.

Little things like that, they add up, and by mid-August Leoma was finished with all the Blinns, including Archie

Perfecting Amiable

whom she nonetheless dearly loved and would forever. But a woman can take only so much, and in her view she had already taken it. What she wanted the day she left was for Archie to come on bended knee and beg her to return home, promising he would clear Uncle Clin out and never ever take in another freeloading relative other than hers. But he didn't come. She recalled every word of their parting conversation when Archie came home for lunch that Thursday. Clin was in the back yard, asleep in the hammock, his favorite mid-day summer activity, when Leoma made her announcement. It was the first time she had seen Archie or any Blinn virtually speechless when awake.

"You're doing what?" Archie asked when he recovered his voice.

"You heard me. I'm moving to the hotel. I'm sure Hollis Beacham will give me special rates for long-term occupancy."

"Long term?"

"You heard me, long-term."

"How long?"

"Until you get rid of that Clin person and swear on a stack of Bibles you won't move another soul in on me to destroy my house and my peace."

"But . . ."

"No buts. I mean what I say. It's them or me. Take your pick."

"But . . ."

Marilyn Arnold

Leoma had then snatched up her suitcase, her handbag, and a book of poetry she bought once but never opened, and walked out the door. She was taking the Toyota Corolla and leaving Archie and Uncle Clin the truck. There were tears in her eyes when she checked into the hotel, and Hollis didn't ask why. Everybody wondered how Leoma had stood it so long. Not that Archie wasn't a dear and didn't give a good haircut. He just had all these relatives that wouldn't meet any decent person's standards for cleanliness or sanity, least of all those of a person with a finishing school education.

Well, it wasn't long after Leoma moved out that Uncle Clin decided to move on. He explained his decision this way to the patrons at Archie's barbershop: Archie was a fine fellow and all, but he was anything but accomplished in the culinary and other domestic arts. Uncle Clin quickly tired of peanut butter sandwiches and Campbell's tomato soup. Besides, he heard there was a widow in the next town who could use a little company, and he was always ready to oblige a lady in distress. The chivalric code was his personal bible. He claimed that Lancelot was his middle name, but no one alive could verify that.

Leoma learned at the Cuts 'n Curls that Clin had left town, and she was waiting for Archie to come for her. There was no reason for him not to, now, unless he didn't want her back. Maybe he was doing just fine without her. Three days

Perfecting Amiable

went by and he still didn't come. Leoma was sick at heart, but she told herself that she had her pride and she'd rot in this hotel room before she'd go home without being asked. Oh, she tried to put a good face on things in the hotel coffee shop, where she found herself saying far too much to Mrs. Ransom, and at the beauty parlor where anything said was too much. Generally, she had the sympathy of the Amiable women, especially at first. But by this time their sympathy had worn thin and they turned to other things. Leoma had never felt so alone in all her life. She drove to Sage a time or two and visited her mother, but she never let on what had happened. A girl with a finishing school education did not cry on her mother's shoulder, especially if her mother was becoming forgetful and wouldn't remember the conversation for more than ten minutes anyway.

At last, Leoma arose from her seat by the hotel window. "Whatever will I do?" she cried aloud. "I can't go on like this, but I can't go home either." It was then that she noticed a piece of paper that had apparently been slipped under her door. "What's this?" Leoma unfolded the paper and went to the window for light. The note told her to go in private to the remaining half of the Carruth house, and there ponder the maxim below. When she had divined the riddle's meaning for her, she was to write that meaning on another piece of paper and leave it at the Carruth place. This is what the maxim said:

Marilyn Arnold

TWO WRONGS CAN MAKE A BLIGHT.

"Who's playing tricks on me?" Leoma demanded. "This thing makes no sense." For several minutes Leoma paced the floor of room 302, staring first at the paper and then at the blind hanging askew above the open window. She was perplexed. Why didn't Archie knock on her door or leave her a note? Didn't he love her any more? Had he given up on her?

Since Leoma had nothing but time these days, she decided to follow the instructions on the note. It was something to do. Minutes later she was pulling into the driveway at the Carruth house. Leoma parked in the shade of the big cottonwood tree, her gaze fixed on the house. She remembered the day the brothers took a saw to it, but she hadn't thought about it in a long time. To her the house was merely an ugly blister on the landscape at the edge of town, something she scarcely noticed any more, like an old cartoon in a yellowed newspaper at the bottom of the box. But now, someone had purposely called it to her attention. "All right," she said, addressing the house, "tell me what I need to know."

Leoma was familiar with the adage in its original form. Who wasn't? "Two wrongs don't make a right." So she focused on the unaltered opening words, "two wrongs," repeating them over and over while the reddening sun fell

Perfecting Amiable

toward the darkening bluffs. "Two wrongs, two wrongs."
Yes, she said at last, silently, there were two people in the
wrong here, Thoral and Thurlin Carruth; and there were at
least two people wronged, their parents. Two wrongs. And
this house, this house is a blight on the landscape and the
town. "Two wrongs can make a blight." Then it struck her.
If only one brother had swallowed his pride and gone to the
other, why . . . ! The revelation came like a thunderbolt.
Leoma grabbed the notebook she always kept in the glove
box and began to write. She had to flip on the Corolla's interior light to finish. Then she made her way to the front of the
house, its inside wall now sadly exposed to the elements,
and pushed her composition between the crumbling foundation and the house frame. That done, Leoma almost ran to
the car, stumbling several times on the uneven turf. With the
door still open, she backed up, slammed the stick into first
gear—closing the door as she went—and raced for home,
laughing and crying at the same time.

The next morning, before he left for the barber shop,
Archie Blinn was seen attaching a rather large sign to his
front gate. It read "NO VACANCY."

Eleven

Every town has its resident grump, and Rural P. Cremm was Amiable's. He was also its chief critic and full-time chauvinist, which is often part of the job description. In his politics Rural leaned so far to the right that he met himself coming back. A proponent of conspiracy theories and an advocate of guns in schools, churches, shopping malls, kitchens, and everywhere else, Rural took his principal pleasures in maligning his neighbors, despising his son, arguing the inferiority of women, ridiculing what he called "soft-belly religion," hating the government, and admiring the arsenal of lethal weapons in his basement. As far as anyone knew, these were Rural's only entertainments. They were enough. More than enough.

Perfecting Amiable

Some found it especially fitting that he was employed as the town's trash collector. He drove the power lift garbage truck and lived with his no-good son Leon Roy in a small green stucco house out at the landfill.

It happened that the landfill was across the highway from the Carruth house. The house and the quarrel that led to its division served as a daily confirmation of Rural's negative view of the human race. It also confirmed his conviction of his own supremacy. He was on hand for the cutting ceremony and openly enjoyed the disastrous conclusion that killed two brothers. That, perhaps more than anything, turned Amiable's kindest citizens against him. A few others probably enjoyed the disaster, too, but had the good sense and delicacy to keep it to themselves.

If Rural was off somewhere or under the weather, the garbage didn't get collected, but stacked up at the bottoms of driveways and in garages. Leon Roy wouldn't stoop to such labor, despite the added benefit of ready leftovers and discarded treasures. The collection days Rural missed were appreciated by the resident squirrels and local dogs, but not by the citizenry. Rural never explained himself, and people didn't dare complain for fear he would pass up their trash when he did make his rounds, or would "accidentally" scatter it across their property. He spit a lot and walked with a limp, but nobody knew why.

Marilyn Arnold

And thus it was that Rural Cremm was actually the most powerful man in Amiable, a kind of de facto monarch. No one dared cross him. Any who contemplated it were brought up short by visions of great trash heaps deposited in their yards in the dark of night. Privately, some loathed him and ridiculed him for smelling like spoiled meatloaf and worse; but in public, in daylight, they did all in their power to keep on his good side, if any side of him could be called good.

Most of the townspeople found it easy to dislike Rural, much as captives hate their captor; and working around garbage had not rendered him more attractive. They wondered what kept Dorsen Ruckles, the mayor, from firing him. Maybe Dorsen was afraid of getting on his bad side, too, or maybe it was his looks. Rural was a fierce-looking, sour-faced man—a short, stocky fellow with green eyes set in a square face. His heavy black eyebrows matched a thick crop of black and gray streaked hair that covered his head and some of his face. The only time his jaw met a razor was when Archie Blinn shaved him every week or so. It was Rural's only concession to civility.

Rural made it no secret that he saw little use for anybody other than himself, and he included Leon Roy in the roster of everybody else; but he was especially down on public servants (never mind that technically he was one), spineless religious people, and women—all of whom he lumped

218

Perfecting Amiable

together as the "walking worthless." People saw some contradiction here because if Leon Roy really was his son and wasn't dropped from some alien space craft to lighten the load, they knew there must have been a woman in Rural's life at least once, some thirty or thirty-five years ago. In spite of that, or maybe because of it, Rural liked to say that the plan requiring women for birthing purposes and children for filling the gap between birth and adulthood was poorly conceived (he would not have appreciated the pun). The whole setup added fuel to his argument against the existence of a wise, all-knowing God. Only adult men—and few enough of them, as the Carruth brothers proved—were worth their salt, as the Lord should have known in advance. Rural argued that women had one legitimate function, giving birth to men. After that, they were a drain on society and a thorn in the side of their masculine betters.

As for the government, well, it was run by a bunch of nincompoops. Rural boasted that at election time he always wrote in the name of Ulysses S. Grant for president and his own dead father for governor. Leon Roy said Rural might as well write in Leon's name if he was hellbent on wasting his vote. Rural, however, would never write in his son's name because Leon leaned almost as far to the left as Rural leaned to the right. These differences did not make for harmony in the home. Leon Roy saw it as his birthright to be taken care of by his father, with the government as backup. At the last

Marilyn Arnold

general election Leon Roy voted straight Democrat, to cover his bases, he said, in case he found himself dependent on the government's generosity. His post-election conversation with his father went like this:

"Why'd ya do that?" Rural demanded the evening after the election as he sat at the wobbly kitchen table polishing the barrel of his favorite shotgun. "Based on that argument, you shoulda voted fer me. I'm the one yer livin' off of, not the gov'ment."

"Some living. The town garbage man and the town dump!" Leon sprawled on the broken down, black plaid sofa picking his teeth with a match stick while he memorized a poem by Ezra Pound. That's what Leon Roy did mainly, he memorized poems and he aggravated his father. He also ate.

"'Sanitary engineer' and 'landfill,'" Rural corrected. "Them's the proper terms. How many times I got to tell you?" Rural gestured to his left. "You ain't satisfied, there's th' door. Nobody's makin' you stay."

Leon did not look up. "Why, I'm adding class to this place," he said with a sneer. "You ought to be grateful."

"Grateful! Sharin' quarters with some bleedin' heart liberal who reads poetry (he pronounced it poh-try) the livelong day an' votes fer them communists? Why, if they had their way, we'd all be in soup kitchens without a gun to our names."

Perfecting Amiable

"Ah, yes, one would not want to be caught in a soup kitchen without a gun, would one?" Leon considered himself an intellectual and tried to talk like one.

Rural paused while that thought entered, traversed empty space, and departed; then he took up where he had left off. "An' we'd have a female for president! I can't think of nothin' worse than a country run by a pack a' females who don't know which end of a rifle t' shoot from. Imagine. A female commander in chief. Aye, aye, ma'am. Hunnh!"

Leon spit out a splinter. "Well, as I've said before, there must have been a time when you liked the ladies all right, or I wouldn't be here, now would I?"

Rural sighted down the barrel at his son. "I've tol' you time an' again how that happened. I was tricked. Them friends a' yer mother's got me drunk and took me t' Las Vegas. When I come t' my senses I was hitched an' you was on the way."

"Yes, and when she came to her senses, she ran off with somebody else." Leon snickered as with some difficulty he pushed up off the sofa and ambled to the multi-stained Frigidaire, one of several appliances Rural had appropriated from the dump. Leon Roy did not have a clearly defined body. Rather, it seemed to spread randomly into whatever space it occupied. If he was indeed supported by the customary structure of bone and muscle, it was not apparent to the casual observer. His father sometimes referred to him as the

Marilyn Arnold

Pillsbury dough boy. Leon rubbed his already tousled brown hair as he stood peering inside the opened refrigerator door. "Where's that leftover pizza from yesterday? You surely didn't eat it all?"

Rural set the rifle decisively on the table. "I bought it, I ate it."

"Are you sure you didn't rescue it from someone's garbage can?"

"Since when'd you git so fussy? The way you look, food from garbage cans is too good fer you."

Leon's clothing of choice was an enormous pair of ill-fitting blue jeans, sandals with a torn strap, and a smudged T-shirt that said in front: "Lyndon Johnson forever." The back said, "Ted Kennedy for now." His father wore khaki fatigues with a hole in one knee and a black T-shirt with perspiration stains under the arms. Each was a walking advertisement for his chosen political views.

It was hard to tell how old Rural was because, as the townspeople said, he was born old. He was old when he arrived in Amiable some twenty-five years ago, and he hadn't changed much since he arrived, physically or in any other noticeable way. Leon Roy showed up five years ago. When his father asked Leon Roy how he found him, Leon said he followed his nose. He meant the smell. People figured that if

Perfecting Amiable

Leon was thirty or more, then Rural had to be fifty at least, and was probably closer to sixty.

Discounting the grumpy old men principle, which usually sets in quite late in any case, people can generally be expected to improve with age, at least in terms of character. Most normal people mellow and ripen in wisdom and understanding as the years go by. Rock musicians, movie stars, professional athletes, and politicians are the notable exceptions, as everyone knows. They are paid to remain juveniles, and for most of them, it comes naturally, with a little help from the surgeon's knife. Thoral and Thurlin Carruth did not become celebrities until they died, but they proved themselves worthy of membership in the celebrity brotherhood by sawing their house in two.

The fact is, Rural's character did not improve over time any more than the Carruth brothers' did. If anything, Rural's character got worse. And no one expected any better of Leon Roy, his son and heir. Of course, Leon had already achieved the virtual stasis of a blimp when he arrived in Amiable, so he was defined in everyone's mind from day one. Furthermore, his affinity for poets like Ezra Pound and Langston Hughes was enough to make a frail person drink cranberry juice, take two aspirins, and go to bed out of fear that what afflicted Leon was contagious. Coral Watters, the librarian, was forced to carry books containing such undesirables because Leon Roy insisted, and she didn't want to be on the bad side of anybody associated, however remotely, with garbage collection.

Out of scrap metal from the dump Rural had construct-
ed a tall, rusted iron fence around the house he and Leon
occupied. Behind its locked gate and multiple "keep out"
signs, all of them hand-illustrated with skull and cross
bones, the low-slung house all but disappeared. Those who
took the trouble to squint through the fence and wild vines,
not to mention the rusty water heaters and old stoves Rural
had pulled from the trash heaps against a future need, could
see a small cannon pointing at the walkway from the crumbling front porch. People liked to think the cannon was there
for decoration and was not loaded, but no one knew for sure.
They were happier not knowing.

All in all, despite the vital service Rural rendered the
community, the truth is he was an embarrassment, a living
contradiction of the town's name and proud heritage of
amiability. Ditto Leon Roy. As such, they were persons
Mayor Ruckles and the women of the Ladies League and
the hierarchy of the Church of the Brethren Revitalized
would like to have kept under wraps. The town had enough
to live down with the Carruth fiasco without the Cremms
adding to the load. Unfortunately, the fence around Rural's
house was designed not to keep the occupants in, but to
keep others out. Not that anyone but a few mischievous
boys and curious dogs had any real desire to invade the
compound more than once. The boys, naturally, wanted to

Perfecting Amiable

get inside the fence because entry was forbidden. "And besides," they argued, "it's dump property, ain't it? We got a right, ain't we?"

Whenever a dog that actually belonged to somebody wandered too far from home and showed up poisoned, or somebody's bicycle disappeared that got left too near the road on garbage day, Rural got the credit for it. He made no secret of the fact that there were few things he hated more than pampered dogs, unless it was pampered children and the women who pampered them.

Since he specialized in trash vocationally, it wasn't much of a stretch for Rural to specialize in it verbally, too, as an avocation, if you will. The problem was Rural had no close human neighbors to enlighten, and his son's politics rendered him a lost cause. Therefore, Rural had to seek out audiences in town and elsewhere. In fact, Sunday mornings, for any who cared to attend, he regularly delivered sermons at the dump that the Lord wouldn't have recognized. The congregation consisted mainly of scavenger birds, gaunt stray dogs, gaunter transients, and the occasional traveling evangelist with grandiose hopes of converting Rural to the True Word. Days other than Sunday, Rural conducted services in a variety of places, with concluding exhortations over beer in Sally's Saloon and Grill. When Leon Roy turned up midway through Rural's last performance at the landfill,

225

Rural threw the book at him. Literally. Rural always carried a Bible and a rifle on these occasions, both of them powerful testifiers, and he wore a black wide-brimmed hat and a moth-eaten black suit coat over his fatigues.

"The Lord made woman to serve man and to bear his seed. They ain't good fer much else," Rural was saying. "They c'd be shot after the second or third child, and nobody'd miss 'em."

"Amen!" shouted a drunken transient in dirty coveralls, waving his bottle in the air. He was Rural's only communicant besides Leon Roy.

"An' the Lord has sanctified guns an' war, at home and abroad," Rural bellowed.

"Amen!" the transient affirmed, raising his bottle even higher—then toppling over.

That's when Leon Roy broke in. "I thought the Lord was the Prince of Peace," he hollered. "It says so right there in the Holy Book, doesn't it?"

Rural glared at him. "Where's it say that? You show me. He's the one tol' me to stock up on all them guns. Hail Armageddon!"

"Hail, Holy Light," Leon replied, borrowing a phrase from John Milton. Leon Roy had persuaded Coral Watters to acquire Milton's *Paradise Lost* for the library, over her objections that Milton was most likely out to overthrow the government.

Perfecting Amiable

That was the point at which Rural snapped and flung his only copy of holy writ at his only son's plump head. His aim was as bad as his preaching and Leon Roy lumbered off unscathed.

"Hail, Prince of Peace," the drunk cried from where he leaned against the barely recognizable carcass of a 1949 Ford.

Rural threw him an ugly look, retrieved his book, and stomped off.

Only Archie Blinn, the barber, had been successful at even momentarily silencing Rural, who seemed to have some grudging respect for the razor that Archie wielded with impressive authority whenever Rural began to hold forth. Although Rural had no shortage of criticism for the human race in general and the citizens of Amiable in particular, he directed his most vitriolic comments at women and his most passionate pleadings on behalf of the celibate life. When people asked Sally why she let Rural and his mouth through the door of Sally's Saloon and Grill night after night, she had a ready answer: "Why, folks comes in just t' hear ol' Rural rant an' rave. Cheapest en'ertainment I ever had. He don't cost me nuthin'. O'ny trouble is, he's hard t' shut up sometimes."

A typical evening in Sally's Saloon and Grill might begin with Rural's entry and beeline to the third barstool from the right. All the regulars knew not to claim that stool for themselves, but if some unfortunate newcomer happened to be on that stool when Rural arrived, it foretold stormy weather. And if that newcomer happened to be a woman, look out. The regulars scampered to a neutral corner and covered their heads.

It was late afternoon toward the end of August when the last woman made that fatal mistake. She was a reporter with a Colorado newspaper that was doing a series of feature articles on small western towns with unusual names. Her name was Dana Zellin, and this was her first exposure to Amiable. Needless to say, it was a memorable one. There she was, in tight jeans, skimpy T-shirt, and black leather vest, on the third stool from the right when Rural ambled through the door, out of bright sunlight into dim bar light. He didn't see her at first, but he was aware people were backing away from him. Rural took it as a sign of respect, until he saw Dana Zellin on his stool.

Sally intercepted him in mid-transit, planting a staying hand on his chest. Sally was shorter than Rural, and probably older, but she was no pushover. None of the local men gave her any trouble. They knew better. "Now, see here, Rural, that there girl's a visitor in town doin' a story on us. You leave her be, y' hear? She'll be outta here in a coupla days. You don't own that there stool."

"Outta my way, Sally," Rural snarled, "I don' wanna

hurt you." He tried to brush her aside, but she held her ground. "No woman of the opposite and inferior sex is gonna set on my stool. You move 'er, or I will."

Finally, Rural pushed Sally out of his way and arrived, arms folded menacingly, at the disputed barstool. Dana Zellin looked up at him, curled her heavily painted lip, and turned back to her sandwich and coke.

"See here, lady," Rural shouted, "that's my seat yer in!"

Dana Zellin looked up again. "Oh, is it? I didn't see your name on it. Perhaps I missed it." She made a big to do of searching the barstool, top and bottom, for an inscribed name, then plunked back onto the red vinyl seat before Rural could snatch it from her.

Rural was so accustomed to intimidating all women, and quarreling with any men who weren't intimidated, that he was confused and uncertain about how to proceed. "I hafta have that seat," he said. "I always have that seat. Ever'body knows it's mine." It was the closest thing to a whine anyone had ever heard from Rural.

"Well, welcome to the real world," the reporter said, smiling sweetly. "You don't have it today because I was here first."

Rural heard a snicker from the back of the room. He jerked his head around, sensing that a lot was at stake here. His reputation. Self-respect. As he turned back, a flash of light assaulted him.

Marilyn Arnold

"Thanks for the picture," the woman said. "This is the sort of local color I was looking for. Are there others like you, or are you one of a kind?"

Furious, Rural lunged for the woman's camera, but she was too quick for him. She hopped off the stool, tipping it on its side; he tripped across it and landed on the floor. Pocketing her small camera and hoisting her bag to her shoulder, Dana Zellin moved to the door in the self-possessed manner of a model on the fashion runway.

"S'matter, Rural," mocked a male voice from a dark corner, "little lady get the best of ya?"

"Maybe if yer good, she'll letcha set there t'morrow," another chided.

Emboldened, other voices joined in, and then all dissolved in laughter. Rural got to his feet and stomped out, leaving the offending barstool on its side on the dark vinyl floor. He was not a happy man, but then he never was. "It'll be a cold day in Hell b'fore I set foot in that place again," he muttered. "The place c'n rot fer all I care." The trouble was, that left him only the Grab sum Grub and the barber shop, and possibly the hotel lobby or the mercantile, as enclosed venues with captive audiences for his oratory. Each of those had drawbacks and less amenable management. A man like Rural Cremm needed a place like Sally's.

Perfecting Amiable

Stinging with hurt and anger, Rural stumbled up the two steps into the dump truck and roared back to his small green house at the landfill. As he pulled to a stop, inspiration struck. He remembered a favorite "Peanuts" comic strip from some years ago. It featured the crosspatch Lucy, whom Rural loved as a soul-mate. That she was drawn as a female did not trouble him for long. He pronounced her name "Lucky," thereby achieving a cost-free sex change for her and a clear conscience for himself. In the strip Lucy goes about among her playmates handing each of them a long list of their individual faults, compiled and edited by herself, traits that in her view need correcting. In the final frame, her mission accomplished, she confesses her reasons for going to such trouble. "I'm just trying to make this a better world for me to live in," she says with a self-satisfied smile. It made perfect sense to Rural, who had never seen the subtle humor in that particular strip, or in any other strip for that matter. Nonetheless, he read the comics faithfully and literally, gleaning tidbits of personal justification from characters like Lucy.

Rural contemplated doing as Lucy had done, cataloguing his neighbors' faults, thereby making those folks unhappy in a more formal, lasting way than he had done in the past. Nobody knew their faults and vulnerabilities better than he because he had made a study of their garbage. Rural always had a hankering to write his criticisms, but without sufficient motivation before. Even now, he didn't know quite how to go about it, but trusted that he would come up with a suitable plan. It occurred to him that he could adorn their garbage cans with commentary and avoid confronting them personally. What the industry called point-of-contact advertising. He might well be the first to publish on garbage cans. Why, he might even start a trend among trash collectors. Another possibility was the "letters to the editor" section of the *Sage Star Review*. As with any newspaper, letters to the *Star Review* were largely submitted by malcontents like himself, some grammatical, some not. The paper's editorial staff seemed to welcome controversy and malice. Rural figured they would print whatever he sent them, no questions asked.

Since Amiable had no newspaper, many of the locals subscribed to the Sage paper, as Rural did, and received daily delivery. A good many others bought the *Star Review* at the hotel or at the Amiable Drug or one of the other local businesses. Rural prided himself on his writing ability, though the last recognition he received for it was in the fourth grade, when his three-sentence essay on the subject of "My Mother" won a gold star from his teacher, Miss Kupfil. That was before he discovered what inferior creatures women are. Now, it hardly seemed to Rural that he ever had a mother, or that he could have been so deceived about women. He knew he could still write, though. He had a gift

Perfecting Amiable

for talking, after all. What's the difference? he asked himself. It's all words. Rural felt a great burden eased. Revenge so cleverly wrought was soul-satisfying. He could go to bed with a lighter heart and a sense of purpose.

In bed with the light out, however, Rural was too agitated to sleep. Lying there in the semi-darkness, fully dressed as usual, to save time and effort in the morning, he weighed the benefits and drawbacks of the two plans. After tossing about for some time under the old tied quilt he'd bought at a garage sale years ago, he sat up and stared at his dusky image in the cracked dresser mirror across from the bed. Rural's mind was abuzz. He decided the newspaper was not the way to go after all. It might be weeks before the editors got around to printing his compositions. And if there was a female among them, his labors might never see daylight.

Then too, how many of his Amiable targets were likely to read the op/ed pages, much less recognize themselves? Not many. Most of them saw no point in wasting time wading through views that did not coincide with their own. But they'd read something pasted on their garbage cans, all right. He'd bet his bottom dollar on that. The decision made, Rural was eager to begin. For inspiration, he padded downstairs into his basement bunker. There he fondly stroked the firearms and ammunition he had accumulated over the years, and the cases of food the weapons were intended to protect.

Marilyn Arnold

Rural was convinced that an attack by either aliens or foreign terrorists was imminent, and he intended to be prepared if they came to Amiable, or if a natural disaster cut off the food supply. It hadn't occurred to him that he could fire only one or two weapons at a time, and that very nearly all of his guns were therefore not only superfluous but could, in fact, be seized by an enemy—or by starving neighbors whom Rural would presumably shoot rather than feed. Nevertheless, surveying his weaponry gave Rural a great sense of peace and power. He imagined himself standing heroically alone against invading enemies, and eating heartily while others less prudent wept in hunger and anguish. He would, however, have to figure out how to keep Leon Roy from devouring his stores without shooting him. After all, it would not do to shoot his own son, except under the most dire of circumstances.

Leon Roy discovered his father the next morning. He knew just where to look if ever Rural was missing when the dump truck wasn't—in the armory, Leon's term for the basement. And there's where he found him, at the bottom of the stairs, asleep between two cases of rifle shells. Not that Leon would try to negotiate the narrow stairway to the house's lower regions. He found standing at the top of the stairs and shouting at the top of his lungs easier and just as effective.

Perfecting Amiable

"Hey, Rural P.!" Leon frequently called his father Rural P. just to get his goat. He said it was gross overstatement to call Rural "father," much less "Dad," which suggested affectionate respect. When Rural protested, Leon always asked what he should call him, then. Rural always said "call me irresistible," after the old song. Then he added testily, "Don't call me at all."

On this occasion, it took three summons before Rural answered his son. "Aw right, aw right," he growled.

"Time to get out and earn our daily bread," Leon Roy called down to his father. "How come you slept among the munitions last night? Did you have a revelation I should know about, or do you find comfort in the smell of gunpowder?"

"My answer to yer questions is, none a' yer beeswax, an' what's it to you?"

"Well, revelation or no, you've got to get out and collect the garbage."

"I ain't workin' today. Got other things on m' mind." Rural stretched and started up the stairs, yawning broadly and scratching his back.

"The Amiable folks won't be happy about that."

"Let 'em eat nails. I got other things t' do." Rural reached the landing and pushed past Leon to the bathroom.

Leon followed him. "What other things? Preach mass extermination of women to the junkyard dogs?"

Marilyn Arnold

"I o'ny preach officially on Sundays," Rural said, entering the primitive rust-stained bathroom and latching the door behind him. The latch was a bent nail. "Big things!" he called from inside.

Leon could see that he needed to change his approach. He was surprised to find himself curious. When his father entered the kitchen several minutes later, Leon Roy was frying bacon. Rural grabbed a chair and made a big show of swooning into it.

"I mus' be in the wrong house," Rural said. "There's a fat Democrat cookin' bacon in the kitchen."

"It's a peace offering," Leon said. "Come on, fill me in. Maybe I can help."

"Now I know I'm in the wrong house," Rural said, sitting at the table. "When've you ever offered t' help with anything except lickin' the spoons and emptyin' the refrigerator?"

Finally, Rural allowed as how maybe he could use some help, and the two of them spent the day composing what Leon called "Lucy lists," terse notes designed to inform select Amiable citizens of their annoying faults and failings. The two conspirators began each list with the same phrase, composed by Leon, of course. It went, "In the spirit of altruism and for the further perfection of Amiable, it is proposed that. . . ." Leon Roy even agreed to make the rounds with his father for the next few days until all the collection routes had

236

been covered. It stood to reason, however, that a good many deserving citizens would, of necessity, be spared instruction. When Leon Roy pointed that out to his father, Rural only grimaced and said, "Their loss. We'll do the ones that count. Some's worse than others."

Leon Roy had no beef with anybody in Amiable other than his father, so he let Rural pick the first targets and determine the content of the lists. Then Leon himself served as ghost writer and editor, making occasional suggestions which Rural ignored. For Rural it was dead earnestness; for Leon Roy it was entertainment—diversion. He had found life rather dull in Amiable, and this little enterprise promised to spark things up a bit. Since he had no principles to speak of, they weren't violated.

"First stop is them Murdocks," Rural said, pacing the kitchen floor while Leon took notes at the table with a stubby, well-chewed pencil. "They got all those children and animals, an' they act happy all the time. Anybody acts as happy as they do, you know there's something goin' on. They're Commies, is what they are, an' prob'ly Mormons t' boot, mark my word. No beer bottles in their trash can. Not even coffee cans! Worse still, Murdock plays with them children when he should be workin'. A grown man! I'm gonna tell 'em t' go t' Russia where they belong." Rural paused.

"Since when is being happy a character flaw?" Leon asked.

Rural glared at him. "Bein' happy in this day an' age means yer crazy," he said, "or else y' don't read the papers."

"Anything more for this one?"

Rural shook his head. "You c'n doll it up. Next let's do that there Ransom woman. Mrs. Know-it-all, drivin' around in that ol' sedan smilin' at ever'body like she's the Queen a' the May."

"Since when is being nice a huge fault," Leon asked, goading his father again.

Rural opened a cabinet door and slammed it shut. "She does it t' make ever'body else look bad! Her an' her superior attitude! Not only that, but she ties all her garbage up in nice bundles so's I can't check it out without goin' t' some trouble." Rural thought a minute. "There's just somethin' about that female rubs me wrong. I don't trust nobody that nice."

"Maybe we should skip her if all I can write is that she's nice."

"No way! We ain't skippin' her. She's a menace, goin' around takin' people cakes'n things. I suspicion she's a witch in disguise. Lives out there with them cats, puttin' hexes on people."

Leon looked up in surprise. "A witch? Now there's something we can get our teeth into." He fell to writing.

And so, when the Murdocks, Mrs. Ransom, and a few others went to take in their trash cans on that particular August Tuesday, they found a litany of biting criticism taped

Perfecting Amiable

to their cans. They didn't know if it was the work of Rural Cremm or not, but assumed so, rightly crediting Leon Roy for the phrasing and penmanship. The Murdocks got a good laugh out of it and dropped the list back in the trash can. Mrs. Ransom merely shook her head and pocketed the list. She knew only too well Rural's nasty nature and his disdain for women and other sensible people. She had also heard rumors about his basement arsenal, but she knew something other people probably didn't know, something she learned because it was her habit to assist people when she saw an unmet need. Earlier in the summer she had been sitting at the bedside of an elderly friend who had lost her husband just weeks before. The woman, Francella Mayberry, had been unable to sleep without her mate of many years, and now she was exhausted and ill.

Mrs. Ransom stayed with her friend into the wee hours of the morning, comforting her, reading to her, and rubbing her crippled feet until Francella finally dropped off to sleep. Driving home through the empty streets, Mrs. Ransom happened to round the corner onto Maple Street as a man hurriedly limped down the front walk of Windeen Stokes's house. Curious and a bit concerned, Mrs. Ransom cut her lights and followed him at a safe distance. When he entered the town's vehicle yard and minutes later drove out in the trash pickup truck, narrowly missing Mrs. Ransom's sedan, she knew who he was. Now, the unusual thing about this, in addition to the hour, was not that Rural Cremm was using the city's vehicle for personal business. He always did that, and everybody knew it. The unusual thing was the nature of the business, and the fact that Rural chose to park where the vehicle would raise no suspicions.

Windeen Stokes made her living at the oldest occupation in the world for women. The law in Amiable winked at Windeen's activities because she never caused any trouble or acted unseemly in public. She kept a low profile, and she never told what she knew. To have done so would have forced the law's hand. As things were, the sheriff saw her as an asset to the community, a pressure reduction valve that probably kept some men from shooting somebody. Mrs. Ransom chuckled all the way home. The man who reputedly saw women as worse than worthless had apparently found at least some limited use for them.

Rural and Leon Roy went about their mischief over the next several days, causing no little stir in Amiable. Every scheduled collection day anonymous messages appeared on eight or ten emptied garbage cans. Most people, like the Murdocks, dismissed the incident as a mindless prank. A good number, however, were offended, even hurt. Pressure began mounting on Mayor Ruckles to do something. He did. He wrung his hands and paced the floor and drafted letters of reprimand to Rural—none of which were sent. Then one

Perfecting Amiable

evening when Rural came out of the Grab sum Grub, he found a note secured to the door of the garbage truck. He snatched it up and drove off, cursing. It appeared that some copycat was trying to horn in on his game.

At the landfill he pulled a flashlight from his work box and opened the folded paper. What was written there repeated the messages received by other townspeople over the summer, only Rural didn't know it. He was instructed, as previous recipients had been, to go to the Carruth house and ponder the maxim printed below the instructions. When he had solved the riddle, he was to write its meaning, as it applied to himself, on a piece of paper and attach it somewhere at the Carruth place. If he did all this, he was promised treasure. This was the maxim:

A SWITCH IN TIME SAVES THINE.

Rural uttered a few undecipherable remarks, crumpled the note and stuffed it in his pocket, then exited the garbage truck and slammed the door. Stomping into the house he found Leon Roy buried as usual in a book of useless poetry.

"What's put a burr under your saddle, to use the local parlance?" Leon asked, glancing up from his book.

"None a' yer business!" Rural retorted, grumbling his way to the basement. A minute or two later Rural emerged with an assault rifle under his right arm and a box of ammunition and a flashlight under his left.

"Whoa, now," his son said, suddenly alarmed. "You don't plan to shoot anyone, do you?"

"Not unless I get a chance."

Before Leon Roy could separate himself from the couch, Rural was out the door, striding with his limp across the highway toward the Carruth house. Leon didn't follow him. There was no point. Rural P. Cremm was not a man who could be reasoned with. He'd come back when he shot something up and got it out of his system. Besides, there was no one to shoot at the Carruth house.

The moon cast an eerie light over the deserted half-building, and Rural shuddered in spite of himself. "'A switch in time saves thine.' Hunnnh! Makes no sense, no sense a'tall," he muttered. Rural knew the old adage this idiotic distortion was taken from. His dead mother used to say it often enough: "A stitch in time saves nine." Rural couldn't see how either version applied to him, and he didn't intend to pursue the matter. What he was here for tonight was to demonstrate his defiance of the note and the writer of it. At about twenty yards from the house, on the driveway side, he raised his weapon, kicked off the safety, and strafed the house with bullets, from front to back, at approximately six feet above the ground.

Perfecting Amiable

Rural felt no sympathy for the Carruth brothers. In his view, they got what they deserved. Whenever the subject came up in Sally's Saloon and Grill, Rural always spoke of them as poor suckers, botching the house job and killing themselves in the process. "They shoulda settled it with a duel, nice and tidy. That's what I woulda done," he said. "'Course I'm a crack shot," he would invariably add. Rural decided to make a full sweep of the house, and he moved to the back where he continued to decorate the structure with lead, not sparing the door. Getting to the far side was more difficult, especially in the dim light. Clumps of weeds and sod had to be negotiated. Rural's game right leg didn't help either. When a briar caught that pant leg, he stumbled and the weapon he was carrying at his right elbow discharged. A sharp pain stabbed his upper left leg as he fell.

Leon Roy had made it clear long ago that he had no interest in his father's evening excursions into town or around the yard. He preferred to follow his own pleasures, which ranged from obscure poetry, to free food, to bed, and back to poetry. Leon was a sound sleeper and often unaware if his father came in late or went out late. He had taken some interest in the "Lucy List" project, but even that had waned considerably after the first day or two. Leon Roy lived quite comfortably in a semi-dormant state. On this particular evening he went to bed at his usual time—early. His father

often prowled about at night or drove into town, so Leon
didn't think much of it when Rural didn't return. Leon had
heard the weapon firing and hoped it was curing whatever
ailed old Rural P. But when Leon rolled out of bed at his
usual time the next morning, and staggered out to the
kitchen, he was surprised to find the coffee pot cold and the
sink free of dirty dishes. He went to his father's bedroom,
and the bathroom, and found them empty. Likewise the
basement, which he scanned from the upper stairs. Puzzled,
Leon shuffled to the front door and looked out. The garbage
truck was sitting there, just where Rural had left it the night
before. Concerned now, Leon poked about the yard and the
edge of the landfill. He called repeatedly but got no
response.

Well, Leon Roy told himself, Rural's on foot and he
can't have gone too far on that bad leg. I thought he had better sense than to stay out all night. Leon decided to have
breakfast—first things first—get himself dressed, and go
looking for Rural. He figured his father was up to his old
tricks, but an uneasy feeling crept into the pit of his stomach
as he left the house. Walking was not his favorite method of
transportation, and it was with difficulty that he made his
way toward the Carruth house. The shots he heard last night
seemed to come from that direction.

Leon was breathing hard by the time he had lugged his
body across the highway and up the drive to the divided

house. Scanning the area and the house, he saw the line of bullet holes along the side of the building. "Looks like Rural P.'s been here," he said aloud. "Rural!" he shouted. "Where are you?" He paused and listened. Nothing. "Dad!" he called, the word feeling odd on his tongue. Circling to the back of the house, he could see the same line of holes there. The uneven ground made the going a bit difficult for the big man, but he kept moving, shortcutting through clumps of sage and wild grass. And then he saw.

"Dad!" Leon screamed. Not ten feet away lay his father's twisted body, in briars and stringy grass matted with dried blood. Leon could see the bloody wound in the inner thigh of Rural's left leg. He concluded that the bullet had pierced the femoral artery. Rural P. Cremm had bled to death, probably in less than a minute. There were signs he had tried to drag himself up, but it appeared he had lost consciousness very quickly. Leon Roy dropped to the ground beside his father's inert form, took the man's grizzled head in his arms and held it tenderly. It was several minutes before Leon realized that he was crying, shedding tears for the first time since he was a child. "Dad," he sobbed, "oh, Dad."

That's how the sheriff found the two of them, father and son, when he arrived in response to vague reports late that morning of possible gunfire out by the Carruth place the night before, a lot of it. The house, the ground, and the body told the story. The sheriff helped Leon Roy to his feet and into the squad car. Then he called for the town's only ambulance to pick up Rural's body. The sheriff took Leon home and told him he'd be by later to take his statement.

When the sheriff returned that afternoon to the green house at the landfill, he had Rural's clothes and flashlight with him. He wanted fresh clothes to take back, so the dead man could be dressed for burial.

"Where is he?" Leon asked, still in a daze, his face tear-streaked.

"He's at the mortuary. You can make arrangements with them. Go ahead and use the dump truck until you can get your own transportation." The sheriff started to leave. "Oh," he said, "I had to keep the rifle and ammunition box for now."

"Sure, keep them. I have no use for them. Live by the sword and . . ." Leon mumbled, staring at the soiled and torn clothing in his hands.

Mechanically, Leon Roy moved toward the washing machine in one corner of the kitchen. He set the clothes there and reflexively patted them. As he did so, he could feel something in one pocket of his father's fatigue pants. It was neither wallet nor keys. Both of those were on the kitchen counter where Rural always put them when he came in the house. What Leon found was a wad of paper. Something stopped him when he bent to throw it into the garbage bag under the sink. He opened the paper and tried to smooth its wrinkles on the counter. There was the mysterious message with odd instructions and a riddle. Apparently, someone had turned the tables on Rural and was leaving him messages instead of the other way around. Again, Leon nearly threw the paper away.

"Somebody's wasted energy," he said aloud. "That old man would never change." Then, almost in spite of himself, Leon Roy slowly trudged back to the Carruth house. He sat heavily on the back steps and reread the message. After several minutes a thought occurred to him. "Maybe I can learn for him," he said.

Leon could see some sense in the first part about switching, changing course, but he was puzzled by the phrase, "saves thine." Saves what of his? Leon asked himself. How did that apply to his father? What was it about the maxim that upset his father to the point that he would march over and blast angry holes in the Carruth house? Sitting there in the calm afternoon, bathed in sunshine and attended by a busy black-crowned sparrow, Leon slowly realized that he himself was the focus of the saying. He was the "thine" that Rural still had time to save if he acted now, if he changed his ways. The thought hit hard. Indeed, Leon was on the path from indolence to destruction. He needed saving, all right. But the purveyor of the message was wrong about one thing. Rural could not have saved his son. If there was any saving to be done, Leon Roy himself had to make it happen.

Yet, in a sense, by his death, Rural may have initiated the process. In tragedy is sometimes the beginning of hope and new life. The sky was lowering when Leon Roy Cremm finally lifted his bloated frame from the Carruth stoop. He had no pen or pencil, no clean paper, but he took a loose nail from the railing next to him and made his way to the front of the house. There, he scratched these words on the exposed interior wall of the divided house, like words engraved on the inside of his own skin: "Out of death, life."

"There," Leon announced to the jackrabbit who leaped when he tossed the nail in its direction. There, in a saving message from Rural P. Cremm to his son, is also a saving message for the town of Amiable, and for every mortal on earth. The message of the house divided. It was a religious message, Leon saw now. As Leon made his slow return back to the house at the landfill, the phrase he had scratched on the cruelly exposed wall kept echoing through his mind. "Out of death, life."

Epilogue

Word got around the town of Amiable fast. By afternoon everyone knew Rural P. Cremm had accidentally shot himself out at the Carruth house the evening before. Some few who thrived on tragedy took secret satisfaction. Others, good-hearted souls, didn't allow themselves that luxury, even though they had no love for Rural, or for Leon Roy either. The mayor, Dorsen Ruckles, didn't know whether to be relieved or dismayed. In some ways he was glad to be rid of Rural, though his conscience would not let him rest in that thought. He had a public concern, too, because the ugly event that accomplished the ridding was most surely a stain on the city. If only Rural hadn't shot up the Carruth house

249

there wouldn't be so much to explain. Why did he have to choose that spot, of all places, to go off his rocker? If this got out, it would bring newspaper and television people, asking questions and making Amiable look bad again. Then, too, there was the matter of the trash pickup. Nobody with any gumption wanted that job at the salary Dorsen could afford to pay him, much less take housing at the landfill in exchange for a decent salary.

Naturally, the accident was the only topic of conversation at Sally's Saloon and Grill that day, where it was thoroughly chewed over along with Sally's sandwiches. It was also topic of the day at Archie Blinn's barber shop, the Grab sum Grub, the bank, Cuts 'n Curls, the Merc, the hotel, and just about everywhere else. The telephone lines among the stalwarts of the Ladies' League came close to frying from overload, at least so Myrtle at the utility office reported when she showed up at the beauty shop for her perm with Leola Baxter. The speculative possibilities of the event strained Delsene Parmley's powers of self control to the limit, she being a reformed gossip and all. By locking herself in her house and unplugging her telephones, she managed to avoid expressing her views to anyone but her cat. It cost her something, though. She had to cancel her afternoon music lessons and take to bed with the aspirin bottle.

Perfecting Amiable

Naturally, there were skeptics and trouble-makers who raised the big "if" questions. *If* it really was an accident, they said. *If* it wasn't suicide or murder or who knows what. Privately, many more raised the "if only" question on the supposition that a suicide or murder would have made a better story, one that could have been enjoyed by generations to come. Still, the real story was nothing to sneeze at. Mortality being what it is, there are few pleasures to match that of being properly horrified at things that happen to other people and not to oneself. Still, the fact that Rural had felt compelled to leave his signature on the Carruth house in the form of systematic bullet holes added a dimension to the story that was unique and intriguing. In the first place, not every two-bit town had half a house sitting there pretty as you please, right off the highway, inviting questions and ridicule, not to mention bullet holes. In the second place, there probably weren't half a dozen such houses in the whole country, let alone one riddled by some lunatic trash collector who wound up shooting himself. Clearly, Amiable was in a class by itself. Who needed to go to Chicago or Los Angeles or any of those places for madness and misery? There was excitement aplenty in Amiable.

But as night approached on the day after Rural's demise, a strange thing happened. One by one, vehicles began arriving at the Carruth house. People emerged from those vehicles, and some were carrying candles. Each new arrival was surprised to find others there. A soft, "What, you too?" or a shy smile were the only exchanges. Arlo and Sarah Blanchard were first to arrive. Then came Lavoid Perkins. Not far behind Lavoid were Coral Watters, LaDessa Payton, and Rilla Ingersoll. The first candles were lit as Merland Swollet and Tyrel Fernley slipped quietly into the half-circle that was forming as Leoma Blinn and Delsene Parmley walked over to join the solemn throng. Each of them wondered what brought the others, even as they wondered what had brought Rural Cremm to this fateful house—though the proximity of the landfill offered a partial explanation. It was assumed that no one gathered to honor Rural. He was not a loved or respected man.

Nonetheless, those attending what might have been termed a "wake" for Rural felt a strange connection to each other—a bond; and they were aware that the others, like themselves, had seemed more at peace over the last weeks and months. Some could even be described as happy. The collective revery was interrupted briefly with the arrival of Leon Roy from across the street, apparently attracted by the converging of car lights at the Carruth house. Leon did not join the circle, but stood off to one side, his head bowed, his hand fingering in his own pocket the message found in his dead father's clothing. As the group stood there, silently contemplating the silhouette of the house against the pale

Perfecting Amiable

evening sky, each seemed on the verge of some revelation yet to be realized. LaDessa Payton began softly humming "Now the day is over," and one by one the others joined in.

They were just finishing the last strains of "Abide with me, t'is eventide," when another set of automobile lights entered the driveway and switched off. In the fading light, the singers could make out the small form of Mrs. Ransom working toward them. Her presence there struck them as even more curious than their own. None of them felt they knew her very well. She had never quite seemed part of the everyday life of the town, though all would admit she was amiable enough, more so than most, perhaps, though in a distant kind of way. She seemed to float about on the periphery, making her presence felt only subtly, observing but not fully participating. Yet here she was tonight, approaching this most intimate gathering of the redeemed as though she belonged with them.

Mrs. Ransom moved past the semicircle and picked her way through the tumbled grass and weeds to the house. She reached up and felt some of the bullet holes, and when she turned back she was seen to wipe what might have been a tear from her left cheek. Taking a step or two forward, onto more certain ground, Mrs. Ransom spoke.

"I need to tell you something," she said hesitating.

"What, what?" LaDessa responded "Why are you here?"

Marilyn Arnold

"Why did you come to Amiable?" Leoma Blinn cried. "You're not like us."

Mrs. Ransom smiled ruefully and shook her head. "Oh, but I am," she said. "I'm one of you all right, only you didn't know it."

The group murmured in surprise.

"Yes," Mrs. Ransom said, turning back to the house. "I'm the reason why this house was cut in two."

The group gasped, and looked back and forth at each other in disbelief.

Mrs. Ransom turned back. "I haven't always been Mrs. Ransom," she said. "I used to be Bess Mumford."

The older among the group gasped again. "Why, you're the girl . . ."

Mrs. Ransom nodded. "Yes, I'm the girl Thoral and Thurlin Carruth argued over. I'm the girl over whom they became bitter enemies. I began the quarrel that never mended, the quarrel that ended in the division of a house and the deaths of two brothers."

Archie Blinn broke in. "But you moved a long time ago. I heard you moved before either of them could marry you."

"I did," Mrs. Ransom replied. "My father moved mother, and me, and my little brother to Iowa to get me away from the Carruth boys. As you know by my name, I eventually married someone else, someone named Ransom. When he died, I returned."

Perfecting Amiable

"But, but . . . why did you come back?" Rilla Ingersoll sputtered.

Bess Ransom bent down and plucked a long piece of grass that had gone to seed. Stroking her face with it, she looked from one face to the next. "Why, indeed? Why do any of us return to our pasts? It may have been that I felt I had some unfinished business to attend to here. Some leftover wrong to right. Some amends to make." She sighed. "But, of course, we can never mend the past. We can only tamper with the future." She paused, then took a step toward the driveway. "And maybe, in the long run, and the short run too, the future is better if left to its own devices." No one spoke as Mrs. Ransom disappeared among the shadows.

Guiding her old sedan onto the highway, Mrs. Ransom was wondering at herself. She had not intended to tell anyone in Amiable who she was, thinking it better to let such things lie. There were, of course, many things she still withheld, things that would go to the grave with her, unless some of the more sentient folks discerned them. It was enough that those who had gathered tonight had in previous weeks come singly and privately to the Carruth house in search of their better selves. She suspected that eventually some few would guess her secret, but would keep it.

There was something else she had not told them. She had not said why she had come to the Carruth house tonight. She wasn't sure herself, except that maybe it was in an effort to jettison a new burden of guilt that was now overlaid on the old one. Rural Cremm, she knew, would be alive if she had not interfered. Who do I think I am, anyway? she asked herself. What is it that prompted me to meddle with people's lives? Pride. It was pride, and I need correcting as much as anyone else. I need to take my own lesson from the Carruth house.

Three days later, a moving van was seen in front of Mrs. Ransom's place. That same day she was observed in the post office, filling out change of address forms. And then she was gone, as mysteriously as she had arrived. On her way out of town, she stopped at the Carruth house and inserted what looked to be a piece of paper under a strip of loose siding. Leon Roy Cremm, who happened to be returning to the landfill after collecting the trash that day, saw her. He never felt the need to tell anyone what he had witnessed.
